TRAPPED

AN ALASKAN ROMANCE

Larry Kaniut

Paper Talk

Larry Kaniut

Anchorage, Alaska

2023

ISBN: 978-1-955728-08-9 (print)

978-1-955728-09-6 (epub)

AUTHOR CONTACT INFORMATION:

Larry Kaniut, 4800 Natrona, Anchorage, AK 99516

Email: kaniut@alaska.net

Web sites: www.kaniut.com

(907) 345-1475

COVER PHOTO CREDIT:

Doug Dixon for cover photo (Fine Line Interiors).
Doug's photo is of a Regal Air DeHavialland Beaver, similar in all aspects to Lane's plane N2803B. We're grateful to Doug for the photo and for Regal Air's allowing us to use it.

BACK COVER QUOTES:

Cliff Cernick   *Trapped*

David Frain   *Brachan*

Ted Stevens   *Cheating Death*

Paul Harvey   *Danger Stalks the Land*

Jack Olsen   *Bear Tales for the Ages*

ACKNOWLEDGEMENTS:

Pam and Jill Kaniut, whose initial interest overcame my objections to writing a "romance."

Granddaughter Sarah Risch for her work on the format and cover.

Grandson Logan Kaniut for editing help.

Randal G. Terry for help editing

My family for their encouragement and support.

Cliff Cernick who called to query, "I'd like to read your novel." He then flattered me with comments about my writing.

Jody Winquist for her untiring assistance in formatting and accepting the challenge of finalizing the book.

DEDICATION:

To all those looking for the fair maiden or the lad
on the white horse...may your dreams come true
and your love last forever.

Table of Contents

The Beginning

With the steady assurance of someone in control the deep throated cough grew in volume and intensity to the steady and characteristic drone of a de Havilland Beaver. Sitting on frozen Lake Hood, the big buff plane idled on the ice. She rested at an angle on her tiny tail wheel and two powerfully built hydraulic wheel skis.

Ears tuned to this workhorse of Alaskan skies, Gabrielle sat transfixed in the cockpit. The blue trimmed, cream colored aircraft thrubbed a steady, near thunderous roar while warming up. The plane's pilot busied himself with switches on the instrument panel.

Gabrielle quivered with excitement. Overwhelmed with the possibilities, she anticipated her first flight in a single engine aircraft. Only yesterday she had queried the air taxi service. Gabrielle was about to experience the romance of the airways and the mystique of the Last Frontier.

Before her, like a giant row of razor-edged cotton balls, rose the ragged Tordrillo Mountains. Nestled in the heart of the Alaska Range they thrust their snowcapped crowns over ten thousand feet into the sky.

Behind her, stretching from the muddy shores of Cook Inlet and stair stepping up into the Chugach Mountains, lay the sprawling city of Anchorage, a boom town spawned by the railroad and gold in 1914. The city perched on a plateau bounded by Knik Arm and Turnagain Arm and back dropped by the Chugach.

Buildings and bustling streets bore testimony of the city's modern day visionaries—some newcomers, others sourdoughs going back nearly a century to Anchorage's beginnings. Aviation nursed that birth to adulthood. Where Anchorage's park strip had once been its airport, the need to fly produced myriad satellite airports including the military's Elmendorf Air Force Base, Merrill Field, private strips, Ted Stevens Anchorage International and Lake Hood, Campbell Lake and Sand Lake.

A number of air taxi services operated out of Lake Hood, hauling cargo and passengers non-stop during peak months. Gabrielle was such a passenger.

Anchorage lay 3200 hundred air miles from her native New York which was rapidly becoming another world in her eyes. She had already learned a great deal about this Seattle of the North. Where its past proudly proclaimed the gutsy, independent "we-don't-care-how-they-do-it-Outside" attitude, the city's face was now global, encompassing peoples of all races, religions and cultures.

Gabrielle yearned for more information about this raw land called Alaska. Eager to explore its borders, she held hope for her opportunity. But she was unaware of the fact that within hours her hunger for more and her resolve would be put to the test.

In keeping with her desires and wanting more photos from the air as much as hoping to assuage her hunger for adventure, Gabrielle had driven her rented car to AirLaska, an air taxi service on Lake Hood, the day before.

Wind gusts raked the snow-covered ground, whipping snow in its wake. An Atlas-like, coverall clad man wrestled a huge container from a plane to the office building, grunting as he pushed it across the snow. His strawberry blonde hair shuddered with each wind gust. Steel blue eyes conveyed confidence and captured everything within his gaze.

While approaching him her mind's eye focused and clicked the shutter, picturing her former Alaskan activities. This was her second trip to the Last Frontier. A few years earlier she'd flown from New York to do a photo essay about the Pribilof Island's seal harvest. She'd been so enthralled with the state's majesty that she determined to return in the winter to sample a different kind of beauty. Perhaps to do a photo piece on Anchorage or Alaska's abundant wilderness.

Gabrielle approached Mr. Coverall and in her learned and practiced idiom said, "Excuse me, sir. I'm visiting from New York. Could you direct me to the proper person to provide me information about flight-seeing?"

Ever helpful, he responded, "Be glad to. Where would you like to go and for how long?"

She curtly answered, "I should like to fly over the city tomorrow. I shall need a minimum of two hours for my business."

Lane thought, "She's a gorgeous chick, but her attitude overshadows her beauty."   He guessed her age at 25 or 26. As he sized her up... and down, he was immediately drawn to her eyes. *They're the most beautiful eyes I've ever seen. I wonder if she's always this arrogant? Beneath her facade she seems eager. In spite of her attitude I've always been one to accept a challenge. Maybe I should invite her to go along with me to Nulato.*

"Flying over Anchorage is a good way to see the city and surrounding area. You'll need to reserve a time with our dispatcher, which shouldn't be a problem. Things have slowed down since our Iditarod dog race activities. A lot of folks outside Anchorage tell us that we're only thirty minutes from Alaska, so if you'd like to get a better idea about the state, maybe you'd like to book a longer flight. I'm guessing our dispatcher would let you ride with me to Nulato for the same two hour fee." He quickly added, "That is if you'd be interested and have the time."

Gabrielle hesitated before continuing, "I should like to know where Nulato is? And furthermore what would a trip of this magnitude involve?"

Convinced that she was a tourist, Lane responded, "Nulato is a village northwest of here about 400 miles. I have a load to pick up. The weather forecast for the next few days is good. I'll probably leave tomorrow. On winter trips involving over 300 miles I usually stay overnight and return the following day so I can fly in daylight. I stay with a friend and his wife there. I'm sure they wouldn't mind your staying the night. But if you're not comfortable with that or if you'd like, we could fix you up with a place in town." He didn't tell her that "place" might be the airport office, which was an equipment storage building.

Ever cautious but always the adventurer, Gabrielle plunged ahead, "It appears that would be a more expeditious means of conducting my wishes. I can work it into my schedule. And I am interested. What opportunities for photography exist?"

Lane replied, "No problem. Between here and there are lots of mountains and spectacular scenery including Mt. McKinley. I be the pilot; you be the photographer. Oh, by the way, my name's Lane Morgan."

Beneath Gabrielle's polished exterior a spark of softness ebbed. Although much more sophisticated than this country pilot, she succumbed to Lane's laid back style. Momentarily surrendering her customary formality, she said, "My name is Gabrielle Lacey."

Then she asked, "What arrangements should I make for completion of my flight?"

"Just be here with warm clothes." Although Lane accepted people at face value, he quickly realized that his openness might be overwhelming to a stranger. "Since we don't know each other, maybe you'd feel more comfortable going to Nulato if you knew me better. My sister's having a get together tonight for friends. You'd be welcome to attend. That would give you a better basis for making a decision on this flight with me. Think it over and call me."

Unwilling to accept the commonness of this man, Gabrielle quickly allowed herself an out, "On the contrary. I have a full day planned."

His happy-go-lucky enthusiasm seldom dampened, Lane replied, "Well, it was just a thought. I'll give you my phone number in case you finish early."

Though she considered him forward and a bit bumbling, her curiosity was piqued. She knew that she had nothing else planned. She was bored by the four walls of her hotel. Gabrielle needed no more time to decide. "On second thought, perhaps I could work it in. What would you suggest?"

"If you'd like, I could pick you up...or I can draw you a map."

Quickly regaining her New York nature which encompassed no little suspicion, Gabrielle vacillated. She asked herself whether it might be better to drive by and scope out the digs before agreeing to let a stranger, a bumpkin at that, take her for a ride! She covered her suspicion, "I have to review my schedule. It would be more convenient for me to take your map and drop by if the opportunity avails itself."

"That's fair enough." Lane drew a map and wrote his phone number on it, "This is just in case you change your mind and want a chauffeur. In that case I be the pilot; you be the passenger."

Gabrielle said, "Very well, Lane. Thank you." With that she strolled into the office, spoke with the dispatcher then strode briskly to the parking lot against the buffeting wind gusts.

Leaving work that afternoon, Lane drove to the family home a dozen miles away where his mother met him at the door with her usual. "Hi, son, it's good to see you had another safe day at work."

"Thanks, Mom." He released her from the hug. Like a dinosaur from Jurassic Park he zoomed toward the kitchen calling over his shoulder, "What's for dinner? I'm starving."

"When weren't you starving? We're having your dad's favorite, fried chicken and potato salad. The dessert I was saving for tonight you ate last night for a snack, remember?"

Just then Kelly entered the kitchen and began setting the table. "Hi, baby bro," she greeted him.

"Hi, Kel. How was your day at work?"

With an elongated sigh she replied, "Stressful."

Just then their father walked in and jokingly teased, "I'll bet sometimes you wish you were a teacher so you wouldn't have any stress." He alluded to his high school English teaching position at Dimond High School from which Kelly and Lane graduated. Their older sister Ginger graduated from their cross town rival, lovingly referred to by all but Ginger as "the school on the hill."

Before dinner was finished, Kelly was answering the door as her guests began arriving. While Lane helped clear the table and fill the dish washer, Kelly noticed a strange car drive through their circle drive and asked Lane if he knew whose it was. He replied, "Oh, I forgot. I met a lady at work today and invited her to your party. She may go to Nulato with me tomorrow. That's probably Gabrielle."

Kelly jabbed Lane and responded, "I love the surprises you spring on me. At least it's not some guy you're trying to set me up with this time. Between you and everyone else, I may be married in mother's life time."

"I'll get the door, Kel," Lane said in hopes of getting off the hook.

Just as Gabrielle reached for the door bell, Lane opened the door, surprised and welcomed her, "Come right in. Hope you didn't have trouble finding our house."

Attracted to his ready smile, easy going manner and kindness, Gabrielle responded, "Your map was very explicit."

"May I take your coat?"

Noticing guests' shoes and boots lined along the wall, Gabrielle quickly became aware of an Alaskan custom. She surrendered her coat and climbed out of her flats. Lane led her into the living room. She felt somewhat conspicuous in her fashionable clothes as most of the guests were adorned in Levi's and assorted casuals.

Lane started to introduce Gabrielle to Kelly and her guests as his mother came into the living room. "Gabrielle, this is my mother, Loretta. Mother, this is Gabrielle Lacey, a flight seeing client. She's visiting from New York and considering riding to Nulato with me."

Lane's mother spoke, "We're pleased to have you in our home, Gabrielle." Jokingly she added, "Hopefully you'll survive the evening. Please make yourself at home. Excuse me; I want to check on my husband. I think he went out to feed the horses. I need to ask him a question."

Hardly had the words left her mouth when her husband Park walked through the back door stating to anyone within earshot, "Does anyone want to see a cow and calf moose? At this moment they're eating the tips of the willow bushes in the back yard." The guests rushed to the kitchen window and looked out. They could see the moose nipping at tree branches where the yard light and darkness met. It was then that Loretta introduced Gabrielle to Park.

Kelly's guests returned to the living room and talked about the highlights of the past few weeks. She made a special effort to make Gabrielle feel at ease while Lane heated water on the stove. He strode into the living room and took orders, "Tea, hot chocolate, coffee or spiced cider?"

Loretta and Park enjoyed the kitchen near the fireplace absorbing the warmth from crackling spruce logs and the fire's ageless, mesmerizing powers. Park sat in an ancient rocker reading a collection of hair-raising adventure tales called *Danger Stalks the Land*. Loretta lay propped up on pillows on the 10-foot bay window seat writing a letter.

While the guests exchanged stories amid laughter, Lane motioned for Kelly from the kitchen. "Kel, I volunteered some of your clothes to Gabrielle. If that's okay, could you show her your winter gear?"

Kelly said, "Sure, Lane." Then she returned to the living room. Her sourdough heritage easily enabled her to loan things. Waiting for the proper moment Kelly addressed her newly acquainted guest, "Gabrielle, Lane tells me you may need some cold weather gear. If you'd like, I can show you some of my things should you need them." Then she spoke to the group, "Excuse Gabrielle and me. We'll be right back."

As they moved toward the staircase, they passed family friend Randy Terry and Kelly asked Gabrielle, "What do you have in the way of warm clothes?"

Gabrielle responded, "All I have is a three-quarter length down parka. The saleslady informed me it would keep me comfortable even at 40 below. I've also got a pair of insulated hiking boots."

Kelly said, "I'm not sure how well the boots will work. Perhaps you'd like to try my new Sorels which are designed for very cold weather. The rubber bottoms grip the ice and shed water. You can use my polypropylene underwear and insulated coveralls. You can try on my coveralls and decide whether you'd like my poly stuff too.

"Some people don't like the itch of wool against their skin. If you don't have a problem with that, I recommend you take my Swedish army pants. They're so warm you won't need the polypro."

Borrowing from others was so completely foreign to Gabrielle that she found the thought of wearing someone else's clothes distasteful. But she'd gotten herself into this. She hid a grimace and smirked to herself when she saw the olive drab surplus pants. She thought, My friends in New York would be appalled at the thought of wearing anything so hideous. Realizing that she could take them without wearing them, Gabrielle feigned appreciation, "I'll include the pants."

Finding the coveralls a comfortable fit Gabrielle said, "If you think coveralls are adequate, I'll pass on the poly underwear."

Kelly offered, "If you wear my insulated coveralls over the wool pants, you'll be totally toasty way below zero. I'm pretty sure my Sorel boots will fit you. They'll keep you warm in any weather. Do you have mittens or gloves?"

"I have insulated gloves."

"You might throw some extra things together in case you get weathered in a few days on the other end," Kelly suggested. "Things like toiletries, extra undies and socks. Not to worry, though, Lane doesn't fly in bad weather and is very conscientious. You should be back from Nulato within 48 hours. I almost forgot, Lane told me you're a photographer. I have extra film if you think you'll run short and it will fit your camera."

Gabrielle thanked her and assured her, "I'm more than adequately prepared," then returned with Kelly to visit with her guests. Gabrielle enjoyed herself during the evening and at length excused herself.

When Gabrielle bade everyone good-bye, Lane volunteered to help carry Kelly's winter things to the car with her. They reached the car and he asked her where she wanted the gear and opened the door for her. "I'll see you tomorrow around 9. It feels like it's about zero now and the sky is clear. The temperature usually drops ten to twenty degrees during the night. It will likely be clear and cold tomorrow. Good flying weather. You might call our office to make sure we'll be going. Good night."

"Good night," Gabrielle said. Then she pulled the door shut, turned the key in the ignition and drove toward the hotel.

When she arrived, she walked to her room and slipped into the bathroom to take a shower. While showering, all kinds of thoughts flooded her mind…*I've no doubt that this is a great state. Half a million square miles! A state map overlaid on one of the continental U.S. stretches from the Atlantic across Texas to the West Coast. Canada borders her on the east; the Pacific Ocean fronts her west. The Arctic Ocean is her crown and the Southeast Panhandle her footstool.*

There's no doubt that Alaska's beauty is unsurpassed. Yet tonight I witnessed inner beauty, a genuine invitation to a home. A warm reception. Caring people welcoming me, a total stranger, as one of their own. Warm friends. A family with strong ties, a sense of humor and a concern for others. Their home is like a Safe Home…a haven for safety, comfort and personal growth. It's a warm, refreshing and wonderful atmosphere.

Hot, comforting water massaged her as her thoughts continued… *This cascading water feels so good. I wonder what a shower would be like in the wilderness?*

She chided herself…*I'm acting like a school girl. This is ludicrous. What's come over me? Lane's family is no different from the other families I know.*

But then she wavered, rejecting this defense against her logic… *No, his family is <u>not</u> like the families I know. The people I know in New York aren't like this. They are upper class and motivated primarily by what's in it for them.*

She thought about her friends and family in New York. Even though they were higher class, she saw them as normal. It was not her fault, or theirs, that other classes were below her. Her circle of family and friends were all confident, highly motivated and "a cut above." The only exception was her father, the most common yet the most loving person in her life. But she'd only seen him half dozen times since Gabe died.

More thoughts assailed her. *Will anything come of tonight? I'll return Kelly's clothes when I get back from Nulato, probably need to get them cleaned. Then I'll fly back to New York and never see these people again...probably never think about them either.*

Gabrielle turned off the shower, toweled off and put on her Donna Karan bathrobe. Completing her nightly ritual, she turned on the night stand lamp and picked up her diary and pen. She walked to the queen sized bed, pulled back the covers and sat on the edge of the bed. Knowing that she would be in for an initial cold sensation from the cotton sheets, Gabrielle slipped her robe off and slid beneath the covers. *Brrrrrr.*

Propped against the pillows she began writing:

Dear Diary,

While arranging with an air taxi to flight-see today, I was invited on an 800-mile round trip for the price of two hours' flying time. I thought it strange that the pilot then invited me to his sister's party.

I can't decide what to think of today's events.

Lane is ruggedly handsome. He's 26 to 28-years old. Probably 6-foot and 190#--a powerfully built man.

Initially I thought him a hick. Dressed in grubby clothes, flying a plane. The stereotype of bush pilots is that they're a strange bunch—delivering anything, any time, anywhere while seldom sleeping.

Yet Lane's grammar, vocabulary, language and manner are superb.

He's very friendly, confident and easy going. He's unlike any man I've ever met. It's almost scary. I'd like to get to know him better but...how will this affect Marcus and me?

Lane's family is equally unbelievable. They welcomed me and loaned me things for the trip.

Tomorrow I leave for Nulato. Maybe I'm being crazy, but I feel I've got to make this trip. Maybe it's the beginning of something good.?!

Takeoff

The next morning a phone call from the hotel desk awakened Gabrielle. It took her a moment to realize where she was. She then thanked the desk clerk and sprang excitedly from bed, grabbed her robe and hurried to the bathroom. She caught a glimpse of herself in the mirror and noticed her normally disheveled morning hair. She also noted a wrinkle across her cheek, probably from a blanket crease. She thought, Oh, great. I wonder how long that will be there?

Gabrielle slipped into a pair of slacks. Then she buttoned her favorite Givenchy blouse and pulled a heavy, matching Givenchy sweater over her head. From top to bottom she wore carefully selected designer clothes. She then called room service.

Anticipating a big day she ordered a monster breakfast, devoid of the traditional links or breakfast steak—Gabrielle loathed meat. She prided herself in the care she'd developed in eating wholesome foods. While touching up her hair and applying a touch of makeup, she thought about her accomplishments in promoting the safety of animals.

She'd just put away her makeup when her breakfast arrived. The morning news kept her company as she ate her meal: fruit slices— apple, orange and pineapple; a plate sized ham-less Denver omelet smothered in mushrooms; rye toast accompanied by gourmet Alaska Berry Products jellies (crowberry, raspberry and blueberry) and salmon berry syrup; a tall, frosted glass of apricot nectar and her favorite, blackberry tea.

She looked at the fruit, sampled a tasteless apple slice and sarcastically thought, I guess that's about as fresh as you can expect when you're this far from America.

After breakfast, Gabrielle brushed her hair again then put her tooth brush, paste and comb in her cosmetic bag. She placed it in her suitcase with her diary. She'd packed enough clothes to get her through a couple of extra days. She slipped into her hiking boots, pulled on her parka and stuffed Kelly's stocking cap into a pocket. Gabrielle set her suitcase, camera equipment and Kelly's Sorel boots and coveralls in the hallway and locked the door.

She rode the elevator down to the underground garage, unlocked her rented Lincoln Towncar and set her stuff inside before jumping into it and starting the engine.

With the streets clear of snow, Gabrielle arrived at AirLaska in minutes. After greeting the dispatcher Gabrielle looked out the window, wondering where Lane was. Her eye caught movement outside. She saw Lane near his plane some thirty yards away, moving about on the lake ice near the nose cowling.

Startled from her thoughts, Gabrielle heard the dispatcher, "The flight to Nulato is a go today. Good weather. If you haven't been around planes much, you might want to go out. Lane's very accommodating and can tell you about his job. He loves his Beaver and calls her *Tundra Bunny*! He can help with your bags if you need it."

Normally "learning about someone's job" wouldn't excite Gabrielle. However she had to admit Lane's job was not normal. Curious, somewhat concerned about her safety in a small airplane and wanting photos, she thanked the dispatcher and said, "I don't have much. I'll carry it out to the plane if that's alright."

"Okay, that'll be just fine."

Gabrielle had to admit that her curiosity was a little piqued by the *Tundra Bunny* moniker. She approached her car, removed her gear, set it on the ground and locked the vehicle. She'd have to make two trips to get everything to the plane. She decided to take her suitcase and camera paraphernalia first.

When she neared the Beaver, she hailed Lane, "The dispatcher suggested I come out."

"Oh, good morning, Gabrielle. I see you made it. Glad to see you," he said with a grin. "I'm pre-flighting the plane, checking it over before take off. In aviation lingo it's called a walk around. Follow me if you like. I'll check our fuel and oil levels, remove tie-down ropes, inspect the fuselage and skis for anything unusual. After completing the pre-heating, we'll be off.

"Do you have any other things I can carry to the plane for you?"

"Just the things Kelly loaned me and my travel bag."

"Okay, as soon as I'm finished here, I'll get them for you."

Gabrielle thanked him and said she'd put her camera to work. Then methodically unzipped different pouches for lenses and maneuvered around the area snapping several shots of the plane, the AirLaska hangar and the landscape beyond with standard and long lenses.

Ten minutes passed before Lane walked across the snow covered ground to fetch Gabrielle's things and return them to the plane. Then he and Gabrielle went into the office. Even though he'd called flight service earlier for the weather, Lane asked the dispatcher about the weather and a couple of other questions Gabrielle couldn't hear. Then he turned to her, nodded toward the door and said, "We're good to go."

When they reached the plane, Lane said, "Getting in takes a little practice. Just step from the tire to the first step, then the second. The door's tiny. You almost have to be a contortionist to squeeze in, but you'll get the hang of it."

Lane helped her aboard, handed up her camera gear and closed her door. He set her suitcase, travel bag, Kelly's boots and coveralls inside the cargo hold. Then he walked to the front of the plane, turned off the engine heater and loaded it. He returned for the cowling cover and wrestled the ungainly, oil splotched blanket into the cargo hold before snapping the cargo net across the rear compartment and climbing aboard.

Lane asked for Gabrielle's complete attention in order to hear his passenger briefing. In a very serious voice he said with command, "What I'm going to tell you could save your life and mine. The information is for your safety and to help you feel at ease. If you don't understand anything, let me know."

Lane covered the operations of her seat belt, her door and the radio including the emergency frequency 121.5; he explained the fuel shut off valve and the procedure for shutting down the engine and electrical system should they make a forced landing, emphasizing the necessity of turning off the magnetos at the very last. He pointed out the emergency locator transmitter (ELT) and the survival gear.

He ended the briefing by stating, "I know there are a lot of things to remember. Don't let it bother you because I've never had a problem. I can remind you of anything if you have a question. You need to know that I will not make any abrupt maneuvers with the flight controls to startle or upset you." Then he jokingly added, "In the plane or otherwise."

Gabrielle's mind was a jumble as she tried to remember each detail.

Lane helped Gabrielle buckle her seat belt, reached across her to check her door to make sure it was tight and helped her pull on a helmet saying, "I never fly without a helmet. I know three guys who would be alive if they'd been wearing one. These helmets have built in radio head sets, so we can talk to each other above the roar of the engine.

"You can take comfort in the fact that this plane can fly even if the engine isn't running. That is to say it will glide a considerable distance. So don't panic if the engine quits...but don't hold your breath because *Tundra Bunny* has never quit on me in the several thousand hours I've flown her."

Noticeably relieved Gabrielle responded, "I'm sure glad to hear that." And reminded of the plane's name, Gabrielle asked, "So, what's with the name *Tundra Bunny?*"

"Oh, that. No doubt you noticed the nose art. My father calls my mom TB for *Tundra Bunny*. He has a ton of nicknames for her and the name seemed fitting for the plane. He asked her if she'd mind if he designed a cowgirl in boots, chaps and Stetson. She liked the idea. He contacted Anchorage artist James Morris who does detailed aviation art. The cowgirl and the name went on the plane." Without further explanation he said, "Let's start this bird and taxi to our departure point." Then he added, "I'm going to open my window and yell 'clear' before starting the engine to warn anyone within hearing of engine start up. Oh, and another thing, I forgot to tell you, but the Beaver isn't known for providing a lot of heat in the cabin. It may be a little colder ride than you're used to, but we'll be okay."

That's when Gabrielle first heard the Beaver cough and come to life, issuing the throaty, throbbing distinct sound of the de Havilland's Pratt and Whitney's nine-cylinder engine.

After radioing ATIS for conditions Lane called Lake Hood tower on frequency 119.1, "This is Beaver one-niner-six-niner Bravo with information Foxtrot. Requesting west with north departure from AirLaska."

The tower granted his request, and Lane powered up the bird, lowered the hydraulic skis and began to taxi toward their departure point assuring Gabrielle, "The ice is three feet thick and there's no danger we'll go through."

"That's a comfort," she said, relaxing somewhat. This small plane activity was new to Gabrielle whose knowledge of flying was limited to commercial flight attendants' telling passengers, "Ladies and gentlemen, please observe the seat belt signs." She was finding it more and more fascinating and thinking it could become habit forming…if she could earn enough from her freelancing to afford such travel on a regular basis.

As they stopped at the east end of the lake near the Regal Alaskan Hotel, Lane told Gabrielle, "I'm going to do an engine run-up before we turn around for take off. Just so you'll know, that's where I raise the engine RPM's to check the gauges and flying controls before takeoff."

After the run up Lane called Hood tower requesting permission to take off, "Lake Hood, this is Beaver one-niner-six-niner Bravo ready for take off."

The controller's voice crackled back, "Six-niner Bravo, you're cleared for takeoff."

Lane answered, "Six-niner Bravo taking off."

Lane slowly advanced the throttle and began a slow turn with his right rudder pedal and pointed the Beaver west. He set the power at 34.5 inches and 2300 RPM for full takeoff. Moving at the speed of a fast walk the Beaver gained momentum until it sped over the snow, a slight rooster tail whipping up snow in its wake.

They lifted off and began a slow, steady climb out. While Gabrielle's incessant clicking of the camera shutter continued, Lane changed the power setting to cruise at 28 inches and 1800 RPM's. Then he radioed the tower, "Six-niner Bravo requests left 270 for altitude northbound."

The tower affirmed his request within Lake Hood segment and asked him to switch to departure frequency 126.8. After the turn the Beaver leveled off and climbed to 2000 feet. Lane explained to Gabrielle that air space rules required their flight path be below 600 feet or above 2000 feet because of Elemendorf Air Base's air traffic, which lay directly in their flight path. He told her he wasn't particularly interested in playing chicken with F-15's arriving at Elmendorf.

They were at mid-channel of Cook Inlet and 2000 feet when the controller called and calmly stated, "Six-niner Bravo, you have two F-15's at 9 o'clock at your altitude and closing at one mile."

Instantly Lane raised the left wing and spotted the two flyboys. They were the same two the tower had told him about shortly before "at twelve o'clock." While replying to the tower that he had the fighters in sight and thinking Those guys are fast, he said, "Departure, six-niner Bravo has contact. Thank you."

Five minutes later the tower called again, "Six-niner Bravo, you have two C-130's at 3 o'clock and four miles." Lane had spotted these sky slugs previously and had been watching them. He acknowledged to the tower that he had them in sight then told Gabrielle, "Those flyboys are all over today. I guess they're on maneuvers." He pointed the big birds out to her and told her he was climbing a few hundred feet to be on the safe side.

Moments later he told Gabrielle, "Look out your window." A couple of hundred feet below them an olive drab behemoth lumbered slowly on a right-north turn, passing from right to left. It had gone a half mile past them when a second C-130 rattled up in its wake, thundering along less than two hundred feet below them.

Constantly taking pictures, Gabrielle asked, "Isn't that dangerous?"

"I assume those guys are just playing with us. They're out here all the time. Some private pilots think they are a little overbearing. Nevertheless it's probably a good thing I climbed three hundred feet, or we might have had an interesting day!"

Springing up below them were Matanuska Valley farms, scattered homes and recreational cabins. They cruised at 110-115 knots and Lane pointed out landmarks, "Off to the right up that valley about fifty miles is Knik Glacier. Off to our left is Mt. Susitna or The Sleeping Lady. That low ridge off in the distance in front of us is the Yenlo Hills. And off to its right, that big white tower way out there a little over a hundred miles, is Mt. McKinley.

"If I start sounding like a tour guide, please tell me; and I'll stop."

Gabrielle said, "I'm somewhat familiar with Alaska, but I'm eager to acquire as much knowledge about the state as I can. You're not boring me."

Then Lane continued, "Since we're in no real hurry and because we have daylight, I'll give you the scenic tour on the way to Nulato. We'll fly by way of McGrath and Unalakleet. I'll point out everything in between. We're now on our way to Skwentna, then we'll follow the Happy River over Rainy Pass Lodge and on through Rainy Pass. After the pass we'll set a heading for McGrath."

The great white silence below entranced Gabrielle. Although unaccustomed to verbalizing her emotions, she *ooohhed* and *aaahhhed* at the magnificence. Pearly peaks thrust their heads up from the valley floor. Myriad trails pockmarked the terrain as shining snow reflected the bright sun's glow and azure skies beckoned.

At length, after considering her independence and living alone in her apartment, Gabrielle asked a question that had been gnawing at her, "Is it customary in Alaska for grown children to live with their parents?"

Lane laughed before he responded. "I don't think so. Kelly's looking for the perfect man and hanging out with our parents. I'm looking to pay off my college expenses and live as cheaply as possible... not to mention that we both love being with our family. Although mom and dad have graciously consented to let us live with them, we pay rent and help out around the place."

"I was impressed with your family. You seem to get along well. What are your parent's occupations?"

"Dad's a school teacher. Loves kids. He always jokes about writing the great American novel after he retires. Says he'll write under the pseudonym J.C. Luvsus. Mom's occupation is the family. Her health never allowed her to work outside the home. She wouldn't if she could. In fact she always said the only reason she went to college was to find a good Christian man, get married and have a family. Dad likes to tease her by telling her that at least she got part of what she wanted in a husband."

Gabrielle said, "I was impressed by the closeness of your family."

"Thank you. We do have a great bond and most of what we do centers around our family's activities. What about your family, Gabrielle?"

In what Lane perceived as a guarded reply she answered, "My mother left my father a few years back. Mother inherited a substantial sum of money from her family, but dad wouldn't think of not working. Mother finally felt a separation was necessary."

Lane was quiet for a moment. An expression of sadness crossed his face before he said, "I'm sorry to hear that, Gabrielle." Pressing her a bit he asked, "Is there a chance they'll ever get back together?"

"I seriously doubt it. But deep down I think mother still loves dad. Dad is the most loving and kind man I know. I hope someday they renew their love for each other, but I think father is waiting for mother."

Changing the subject, Lane told her they would begin a gradual climb to altitude for clearing Rainy Pass, "After that we'll let down and maintain a watch for game on the ground and other aircraft."

An hour into the flight Lane asked Gabrielle, "Would you mind digging out that cooler behind me? Mom put together a lunch and some drinks for us. I'll give you first pick since I eat anything."

Gabrielle expressed some surprise and appreciation, "That was considerate of your mother. I don't mind if you choose first. Actually I brought some things to eat. I've developed certain eating habits."

"That's okay. Mom always packs me a lunch, and frankly I was raised to respect women. Since there's only one woman in the plane, please be my guest. Choose anything you'd like." He joked, "Even if you are paying for the flight."

Gabrielle opened the cooler and discovered leftover chicken, potato salad, chips, cookies, vegetables and pop. She told Lane of the variety.

Lane commented, "More choices. Now we have to choose between white and dark meat. You still have first pick."

Ever pleased with her vegetarian diet, she proudly stated, "Since I don't eat meat, that will give you more food to eat."

Lane took her comment in stride and said, "Okay, Gabrielle. I guess I'll have to suffer my chauvinistic stereotype. Is there a back or wing waving at you?" She handed him a back and he thanked her.

Gabrielle ate some of the food she'd brought. She told Lane that she loved the potato salad. Just as Lane was thanking her on his mother's behalf and enjoying another piece of chicken, Gabrielle spoke up. She was staring out at the white silence and nibbling on an orange while sporadically clicking more pictures, "What's that down there?"

Lane turned the yoke to the right, lowering the wing and allowing him to look out the window. He saw a pack of wolves chasing a moose. He explained the scene below and how often it is repeated every week in Alaska. "That pack of seven wolves is probably a family. In the winter they run along on the surface of the snow behind or beside a moose while it breaks through because of its weight. They bite chunks of hide and muscle from it, gulping down the meat and gradually weakening the animal until they kill it.

"Frequently a pack stations itself at intervals so that the wolf chasing the moose essentially herds it toward another wolf in waiting.

That wolf takes up the chase while the first wolf rests, and the process goes on until the moose is exhausted.

"A pilot friend watched a wolf pack chase a moose and hamstring it near Willow. Hamstringing is where severing a tendon or tendons in the rear leg cripples the animal. The snow was so deep and the moose was injured to the point it couldn't move. So it leaned against the snow bank. Wolves fed on it then lay a few yards away. They continued eating on the suffering moose—gulping down warm meat. It took a couple of days for the moose to die. Few have witnessed such savagery; and few can stomach it."

Gabrielle expressed shocked disbelief, "Isn't that unusual? It's my understanding that wolves consume the weak and old animals."

"Well, you've probably heard that in New York. Some people say that wolves kill the weak, the lame or the old which keeps the herds strong. But that's not true. Wolves kill any animal they can haul down. Often dozens. Sometimes the pack devours only the tongue. It's not uncommon for a pack to leave dead prey entirely untouched."

"But aren't wolves an endangered species?" Gabrielle asked. "I've heard there are only a few thousand in Alaska and that hunters and trappers kill around one to two thousand a year."

"There again, people are being pedaled incorrect information. There are approximately 8,000 wolves in Alaska. They're actually on the increase."

For the next several minutes Gabrielle was silent, staring pensively out her tiny, triangular window.

"Before you know it we'll be out of the mountains," Lane said. "I'll set a compass heading for McGrath. Between here and there we'll be flying over low country and frozen swampland. We may see wolves or bison from the Farewell herd. We'll stop in McGath for a break and a restroom stop. Then it's off to Unalakleet before setting a course north along the Yukon River to Nulato."

After a standard landing and take off from McGrath the Beaver cruised along with Lane answering Gabrielle's myriad questions. Then Lane said, "That knob below us is called Old Grouchtop, and just ahead is Bullfrog Island in the Yukon River. Just after that we'll see Unalakleet. On the return trip we'll go from Nulato to McGrath and Anchorage."

Although the steady drum of the reliable Pratt & Whitney R-985 radial engine created engine heat, very little was transferred to the cockpit. Even though the occupants felt secure in the engine's constant purring, the cabin cold provided little comfort. While enjoying the tail end of the flight, Gabrielle wistfully wondered about the remainder of the trip, fantasizing somewhat about what lay ahead.

Sprawling across the horizon from left to right on the Beaver's windscreen lay the vast surface of the Yukon River.

"There she is," Lane said, "that's Nulato across the river."

Gabrielle's eyes lit up, "So, that's the mighty Yukon River? It's really expansive," she said excitedly.

"Yes, it's quite a body of water. You can see the old town site below the new one which is on the hill above. The airstrip is up there too. Kind of like landing on an aircraft carrier."

As the Beaver descended and Gabrielle took in the sprawling, frozen river below, she busied herself capturing scenes outside and inside the plane with her camera. She watched Lane reach with his strong, heavily-veined right hand while he dialed in frequency 122.9 and advised local air traffic of his intentions, "Nulato traffic. Beaver one-niner-six-niner Bravo inbound. Ten miles east. ETA and touchdown on zero-two, ten minutes."

Lane maneuvered the craft to intersect the crosswind leg in the pattern and explained to Gabrielle, "Aviators enter the pattern at a 45 degree angle so they can see and merge with any other air traffic. On little used strips we use the CTAF frequency, an acronym for Common Traffic Advisory Frequency."

He then turned left in his downwind leg prior to turning base. He checked his carburetor air temperature gauge for any ice buildup and to assure proper fuel flow. With skill stemming from thousands of hours of experience Lane methodically reached for the flap lever and pumped down the hydraulic flaps on the plane's wings to provide slow flight and maneuverability for landing. As he turned base, he lowered the flaps to the landing position then turned left on final.

As the Beaver settled over the runway, Lane jockeyed the rudder pedals keeping the wings level and the plane in line with the runway. Just before touchdown he pulled back on the yoke, flaring the plane and gently settling onto the runway. The wheel skis kissed the earth and hissed to a slow roll over the ice covered gravel.

Lane taxied to an area used for transient parking and shut down the Beaver. As Gabrielle prepared to get out to stretch her legs, he said, "You may need to walk slowly along the plane and use it for balance just in case your legs aren't working yet." After she was free of her helmet and harness, he helped her on with her coat.

Lane exited his side, walked around the nose and opened Gabrielle's door. He helped her down the steps to the tire and said, "Just so you know, cold metal can freeze your flesh. Make sure you have your gloves on so you won't injure your hands if you touch the plane."

While Lane placed the helmets on the seats and secured the yoke with a seat belt, Gabrielle clicked away with her camera shutter. He grabbed the engine cover from the cargo hold and wrapped the cowling aft of the propeller to help retain heat and insulate the engine from the cold. Last he went to each wing and secured the tie down ropes before tying down the tail.

Lane looked at Gabrielle and asked, "Ready to meet my friends?" She shook her head in agreement. Just about then they heard the unmistakable high pitched whine of accelerating snow machines.

Bret and Mary bounced across the flat, kicking up snow in their wakes. Ever the confident rider, Bret spun up beside Lane just ahead of Mary. They rose off their idling machines and Lane introduced them to Gabrielle. He thanked them for providing them lodging for the night and told Gabrielle they were two of the local school teachers.

"So far, Gabrielle has survived the trip and hasn't run out of film. I'm fantasizing that her photos and article are going to make me a famous Alaskan bush pilot; but maybe she's going to blackmail me with them."

Gabrielle noticed that Bret and Mary were in their late twenties and they explained that they had been there two years.

Mary said, "I hope you don't get too cold, Gabrielle. We've had a normal winter, but 40-below may be a bit out of the norm for you."

Gabrielle thanked her and said, "You might say it's abnormal. I'm used to cold winter weather around 30 degrees."

Bret secured their things on the machines and said, "Lane, when you called this morning, Mary thought it would be nice to give Gabrielle a tour of town and stop for some groceries. Gabrielle and Lane, you've got your choice of dinner—tacos or pizza; pizza or tacos...unless you'd prefer split pea soup." While they considered his offer, Bret added, "I'm just kidding about the soup because I hate it."

Lane straddled Bret's machine and reached his arms around his friend, and Gabrielle climbed behind Mary on hers. Mary said, "Hang on tight," and they were off.

Their whirlwind tour of town took twenty minutes. Then they stopped for groceries at H and H Enterprises. Gabrielle grabbed her camera for more pictures. Inside the store she and Mary went one way, the guys the other.

When hardly out of earshot Mary told Gabrielle, "You couldn't fly with a safer pilot." Then she asked, "What do you think of Lane?" Without giving Gabrielle a chance to answer Mary plunged ahead, "He's such a hunk. If I weren't married to Bret, I'd figure out a way to get Lane to fall for me. He and Bret were high school jocks. Lane turned down a full ride to UCLA to play volleyball so he could go to a small school in southern Cal that offered his major."

"I've only known Lane twenty-four hours," Gabrielle said. He's a kind, considerate guy. Handsome too. But I'm engaged."

Gabrielle had just removed her gloves, and Mary said, "Oh, I didn't even notice your ring. Anyhow, whoever gets Lane will be one fortunate woman. That guy's something special."

Bret raised the same issue, "Wow, Lane, Gabrielle is pretty darn good looking. Gorgeous eyes and hair. Dynamite figure—like a model. What's up? Think anything will come of it?"

Lane grinned, "On the way up I asked her to marry me."

"You did? Boy, you sure don't mess around."

"She's got beaucoup bucks," Lane continued. "I figured she could put me through my masters and doctoral programs. Then if our marriage goes on the rocks, at least I got my college paid for."

"Lane, I know you better than that. You're holding out for the perfect woman. Tell me the truth."

"She's attractive alright. She's definitely out of my league. When it comes to sophistication, compared to me she's in the stratosphere. Sure, I've enjoyed my time with her. But you know, this trip is not a date. It's business."

Remembering that Gabrielle was a vegetarian, Lane told Bret, "Oh, by the way, you might tell Mary in private that Gabrielle doesn't eat meat."

Calling on her earlier option of tacos or pizza Gabrielle decided on pizza, and they picked out necessary ingredients, found the guys and headed for home.

Bret and Mary's modest home was furnished in pinks and pastels, with a pig theme. Mary told Gabrielle she adored pigs. It started, she said, when she visited Lane's parents one day. Lane's family had bought his dad a piglet for Father's Day, and Mary had loved pigs ever since.

Accustomed to Park Avenue décor—not farm animals—Gabrielle was less than impressed. Hers was a more sophisticated world.

Mary said, "Let's go into the kitchen and see what kind of trouble we can rustle up."

Once in the kitchen Lane handed Mary a cardboard box, "From Los Anchorage. Thought maybe you could use it."

Mary opened the box and beheld fresh bananas, apples, grapes, tomatoes, lettuce and bell peppers. She squealed and hugged Lane, "Oh, Lane. You didn't need to do that."

"Careful, now, Mary. You're going to jump around and knock the box over and damage the surprise on the bottom," he teased.

By now Bret's curiosity got the better of him. While digging for the bottom he helped Mary set the fruit and produce on the counter. At the bottom of the box was a wrapped package. They opened it together as Lane said, "I know you guys love white chocolate, so I spent half my savings from last year to buy you some."

Mary gave Lane another hug and Bret said, "I've always said that it pays to have a pilot for a friend. And in your case I should add, a RICH pilot."

"I'll give you my wealth if you'll pay my college debts," Lane said.

Gabrielle was surprised that Mary made the pizza crust from scratch. Mary rolled it out while Gabrielle sliced peppers, tomatoes and mushrooms. Bret chattered away while he and Lane rattled around with plates and silverware. Mary garnished the pizza crust, making one Canadian bacon and one all-veggie.

Bret gave the diners a choice of grape juice from frozen concentrate, soda or hot drinks in the form of cider, tea or coffee.

They sat around the kitchen table making small talk until Mary served the piping hot pizzas. Bret offered a prayer of thanksgiving, "Our Heavenly Father, thank You for Your goodness and grace, for granting a safe trip to Lane and Gabrielle. I ask that You watch over them on their return to Anchorage. A-men."

While Bret cut the pizzas, Mary asked Gabrielle, "So what brought you to Alaska?"

"I'm a free lance photojournalist," said Gabrielle in her formal style. "I was here previously on assignment, so to speak, and I did a piece on the Pribilof seal harvest. I deplore killing of animals. I wanted to expose the traditionally brutal harvest to do my part in helping stop the slaughter. I was so captivated by Alaska's grandeur that I wanted to return to see what it was like in the winter. It's really like no place I've ever been. Even though I've spent less than two weeks here, I love Alaska."

Bret had witnessed the seal harvest also and knew that only non-breeding males were harvested. He remembered the humane way the seals were clubbed, crushing their fragile skulls and killing them instantly. He knew their management was closely watched. But rather than creating friction, Bret chose to ignore her comments and said, "It's neat that you've enjoyed Alaska. Maybe you'll have time to come again and stay longer. That way you could see and experience this vast country."

Curious about Bret and Mary, Gabrielle asked, "Besides teaching school, what takes up your time during the week? And how often do you get to civilization?"

The others laughed at her comment about civilization, causing Gabrielle to blush. Mary answered, "We travel Outside at least once a year...either in summer or at Christmas. We miss our families, but our lives are so busy here we don't get bored. We have school and community functions, plus we snow machine, hunt and are involved in church activities."

For the duration of the meal they made small talk and visited. The longer they visited, the more relaxed and comfortable Gabrielle became.

After dinner they cleared the table. Lane complimented Mary, "That was the best meal I've had since I was here last time." Jokingly he added, "Don't tell mom I said that."

Mary said, "Oh, Lane, you say that every time you come."

"Okay," Bret said, "you have your choice of watching a video or playing Monopoly outside in the snow."

Obviously it was a no brainer; but Lane said, "So, what Hollywood creation are you going to subject us to?"

"You have a choice," Bret replied, *It Could Happen to You* or *While You Were Sleeping.*"

Lane took a quarter from his pocket, flipped it in the air and said to Gabrielle, "Call it." Before she could open her mouth, he teased, "You lose. Too slow." He turned to Bret, "Let's make it Sleeping, I think Gabrielle is the dreaming type."

Gabrielle surprised herself, punching Lane in the arm and stating, "Actually, Mr. Bush Pilot, *While You Were Sleeping* is my favorite movie. I'm glad you picked it...even though I also like *It Could Happen to You.*"

After the movie they spent the remainder of the evening talking and joking about life in general and in the Bush in particular. Lane asked Bret if he could borrow his snowshoes to use as a model for a set he wanted to make.

Bret said, "You're welcome to them. I commissioned Ivan to make me two more pair which I should be getting any day. By the way, remember that horse trough Ginger sent us as a wedding gift joke? Since she now has her own place and her equines, we want to send it back to her. Even though she's living in Los Anchorage, we thought we'd send it with a note kidding her about adjusting to life in the boonies. Do you think you'd have room on this flight?"

"We can take it down in the morning and see what my cargo is. I'm sure we can squeeze it in. Let's give it a try."

At length Bret said, "Well, it's about time to hit the sack. Lane, would it be too much of an imposition for you to sleep on the couch? We'll give Gabrielle our extra room."

"No problem, Bret. I've slept on worse than your couch. It's a privilege to have it."

Mary took Gabrielle to the guest room and told her, "I'll leave the hall light on in case you need to get up during the night to use the bathroom." Then everyone turned in.

Gabrielle crawled into bed with her diary and jotted her thoughts.

Early the next morning Gabrielle awoke to the aroma of coffee and friendly chatter. She crept from her room to the bathroom, happy to discover it was unoccupied. In a short time she was dressed and strolled into the kitchen where she found the others.

Lane noticed her immediately and said, "Well, Angel Eyes, you look like the princess who slept in the warm water bed in the castle; and I feel like the knight who slept in his coat of mail on the dungeon's cold floor. Just kidding. How did you sleep?"

Again Gabrielle surprised herself and wondered in her whimsy if Alaska's spirit was rubbing off on her. Her eyes sparkled as she purred, "Mahvelous, your knightship."

Lane replied, "Good. You weren't too cold?"

"No, I was actually very comfortable."

As they sat to the table, Gabrielle was impressed by the spread before them—poached eggs, toast, juice and Sunday hot bread.

Lane informed Gabrielle that he had already gone to pre-heat the plane, called the weather service and secured his cargo. He said, "After breakfast we'll head for the airstrip and take off. Should be in Anchorage by late afternoon."

Following breakfast, Bret and Mary dropped them at the Beaver on their way to school. Bret said good-bye and Mary added, "It was nice seeing you as always, Lane. And it was really nice meeting you, Gabrielle. Maybe we'll see you again sometime."

Gabrielle responded, "Thank you for your hospitality." Even though she didn't think being in Nulato again was likely, she had enjoyed it and said, "I very much enjoyed my stay and I do hope to see you again."

Lane turned to Mary and added with a mischievous twinkle in his eyes, "As usual, it was a boring time. I'm disappointed it wasn't Monday so we could watch football. I know you're upset, Mary, since you love the sport so much."

Bret added, "Actually, Lane, she's understanding it better."

At that Bret and Mary skittered off on their powerful machines. Lane turned off the plane's engine heater, removed his cowling cover and stored both in the Beaver before helping Gabrielle aboard. Before they knew it, Lane and Gabrielle were in the air and Anchorage bound.

Remembering what she had said about deploring killing, Lane said, "I want to apologize about our cargo. I didn't know or I could have told you when I invited you to come with me. We're hauling pelts trappers are sending to fur buyers. The season's almost over, but more furs will be coming in later. I'll probably be coming back in a month or two."

Realizing that Lane had no control over his load, Gabrielle stifled her annoyance, "I appreciate your thoughtfulness about my feelings. Even though I strongly oppose the entire industry, it's ironic that I'm riding with a load of dead animal skins. I can't fault you for that, Lane." She tried to play down her disgust, "I'll just hold my nose back to Anchorage and pretend we're hauling strawberries."

Lane said, "I'm sorry about the smell. It takes a little getting used to. We can always open an air vent. It's not much warmer in here than it is outside anyway."

Before long Gabrielle was busy with her camera on another gorgeous, blue-sky day. The scene below resembled a large, glistening white blanket covering hundreds of various shaped pointy lumps, their bases dimpled with gullies and patches of blue-black trees. She wondered about the snow depth as her camera captured mountain contours, river courses and a panorama of dazzling, fleeting scenes.

A Change in Plans

The return trip seemed much quicker. Gabrielle expressed interest in the airplane and asked questions about the different "buttons and things." Lane explained some gauges and major levers including flaps, throttle and propeller. And he told her of the necessity of following procedures that did not overstress the aircraft. He demonstrated map procedures for pinpointing the aircraft's location and talked a little about pilotage and dead reckoning.

Lane called on the radio for weather at Rainy Pass and was told that the pass was socked in. He told Gabrielle they'd try to sneak through the Alaska Range at Shellabarger Pass and see a little different terrain than on their outbound trip. He turned the Beaver and flew up the Dillinger River, noting clouds ahead. He'd done a lot of scud running and actually flown through some hairy stuff alone, but he would never take a chance with a passenger.

He told Gabrielle, "We'll fly a bit longer to see what develops. If we can't get through the pass, we could either go over the top or return to McGrath."

Though glacial beauty and raw nature beckoned, the distant siren song belied the intrinsic dangers lurking below. Lane knew that sky busting peaks dissected by gaping gorges littered the landscape ahead. And the greater danger of unseen wind shears, violent shifts in wind speed or direction, dominated this region. It was no place to park a plane. Noting the need for safety and knowing that altitude would provide a margin of error with a glide range, he climbed.

Within a few minutes it was obvious that the weather ahead was too great a barrier, and Lane started a wide turn toward McGrath, telling Gabrielle they'd land, wait out the weather and check their fuel.

Sitting in the 4-foot wide cockpit the couple endured the chill in the bucket type seats. Gabrielle was giddy in her recognition of landmarks from the day before. The flight was routine until suddenly and without warning, the engine coughed.

It coughed a second time...then it quit.

As the thundering engine noise abruptly stopped, Gabrielle sat in stunned disbelief. She watched in horror as the propeller windmilled without power, generating no thrust. Staring at Lane, her horror-filled eyes seemed to be asking a multitude of questions. Fear gripped her. Involuntarily she blurted, "Oh, my God! Lane! Are we going to crash?"

Lane talked to her in a reassuring voice, "It's okay, Gabrielle." He hit the ignition switch and said, "I'll get her re-started. Trust me, I avoid plane crashes. They could ruin your day."

For the bush pilot who knows his aircraft, the absence of sound breeds alarm.   But that great big, loud silence is taken in stride by bush pilots with any amount of stick time. And such was Lane.

As was his habit, Lane always watched for the safest place to land in an emergency. Quickly he scanned the land below for that spot in the event he could not re-start the engine. He picked a stretch of river between two bends. Then he mentally ran through the engine failure checklist, rapidly scanning the gauges. He affirmed the fuel was on. He checked the fuses and circuit breakers. The primer lock on the fuel feed was okay. He checked the mag switch and tried the ignition switch again. The engine cranked but would not fire, nor start.

Lane switched radio frequencies to 121.5, the emergency frequency, and radioed a Mayday. He spoke calmly in order to reassure Gabrielle and because he hoped he could re-start the engine.

Speaking into the mike Lane called, "Mayday. Mayday.   This is Beaver one-niner-six-niner Bravo. Engine failure. Approximate latitude: 62 degrees, 40 minutes; longitude 153 degrees, 10 minutes. Between Dillinger and Little Tonzona rivers at mountains."

There was no response. Lane repeated the message.

Because re-starting the engine looked grim, Lane's two greatest concerns were whether his message had been heard and the nature of the snow and ice on the frozen river below. He was confident that he could bring *Tundra Bunny* in safely. He knew that if rescue wasn't soon in coming, they'd need a safe shelter.

Conventional wisdom dictated that a downed pilot stay with the ship. He knew if they weren't rescued by spring, that water and weather would melt the ice. If the plane was on the ice, it would sink. Losing the plane would be costly to recover and it would reduce their chances of being sighted. He determined that as soon as the plane slowed, he'd beach it before she lost her momentum.

Then he told Gabrielle, "It doesn't look like she'll re-start. We're going to be fine." He reminded her of the emergency procedures he'd gone over with her that morning and showed her the fuel selector and the master switch. Then he said, "If for some reason I'm disabled, you'll need to turn these off. Do you remember how?"

Trying to hide the fear that gripped her and wanting to believe he had things under control, she nodded her head in assent. She looked at the master switches and remembered the fuel selector had four positions—off, front, center and rear.

The landing spot necessitated Lane's dropping as much altitude as possible in order to hit the beginning of the landing area. He pumped the flap handle up and down until the selector read landing. He lied when he told her, "I've got plenty of room." Then he said, "It's real important that your harness and helmet be secure. In the event we smash into something, your door is less likely to jam if it's open. You won't fall out. When the time is right, I'll tell you to open your door. The slipstream will hold it open a crack."

To reassure her he said, "It will help if you can relax. I be the pilot; you be the passenger. We'll make it."

Lane called upon all the skill he'd acquired and whispered a silent prayer for their safety. He turned the trim wheel pitching the plane slightly nose high to slow the craft. He was gliding just above stall.

Since a plane on skis has no brakes and must rely on friction to stop, Lane's concern was whether there was enough snow to slow the plane or whether the wind blown ice would contribute appreciably to its momentum. He knew the importance of touching down at the start of the straight stretch to utilize its entire length.

Five hundred feet above the river Lane told Gabrielle to take hold of the door handle. Glancing below he could tell the wind blown river ice was pockmarked with snowdrifts. He couldn't tell how high the drifts were but assumed four to six feet.

Lane knew the danger of a violent or uncontrolled landing. In ground strikes of severe force a Beaver's gear usually rips off, often puncturing the belly tanks or cart wheeling the plane. And it was not unheard of for the big birds to burn. He also knew that a major problem for the Beaver on floats experiencing hard landings was for the float supports to collapse causing the floats to smash up beside the doors, trapping the occupants inside. He had lost a flying friend in just such a hard landing.

Not wanting to concern Gabrielle unduly, he hoped that merely a roller coaster ride awaited them. He feigned calmness, "It could be a little bouncy."

Running his hands over the switches Lane turned off the fuel supply, then the radios, next the ignition and last, the master switch. He said, "You won't need to worry about turning anything off."

Moments later just as he pulled back on the yoke Lane shouted, "Open the door!"

Gabrielle opened it and the slip stream held it against the fuselage.

The plane touched the ice and Lane pumped his feet on the rudder pedals turning slight angles right and left to keep the fuselage parallel with the river bank and to give himself a view out the side windows. He hoped there were no obstructions on the ice.

The hurtling Beaver skidded over the ice, slashing and slicing along. Lane looked through his side window on one turn and noticed the first snowdrift just ahead. It looked like it was three feet high. He told Gabrielle to brace herself. They hit the drift and snow sprayed skyward, shooting past their windows. A maelstrom of gyrations engulfed the plane.

Then they were back on snowless ice skidding slower. With bulldog tenacity Lane gripped the yoke, fighting to control the plane's lurching. He pushed first the right rudder, then the left, constantly looking out the windows for any obstructions.

There were more drifts, more snow sailing up and momentarily obscuring their view and the plane's return to the wind blown ice. The plane bucked. Every time it plowed through a drift, the plane shook and shuddered. Violently the wings rocked up and down and the plane rolled from side to side each time they hit another drift.

Lane had more control of the craft than a rodeo bull rider on his mount, but not much. He fought the controls, constantly hoping the gear would stay intact...thinking all the time, "So far so good."

Gradually the plane slowed. Preparing to beach the bird, Lane pushed on the left rudder, and the plane turned toward the bank and a snowdrift on the beach. He noticed a lump ahead, too close to avoid. He shouted, "Hold on!"

Suddenly the left ski slammed into the lump, a snow-covered log. The Beaver shot skyward, tilting crazily to the right. Its right wing tip smashed into the ground.

A split second later the tail struck the ground so hard that the nose shot forward and down, catapulting the tail upward. It appeared the plane would nose over. The force threw Lane and Gabrielle forward against their harnesses.

The nose struck the ice. There was a crashing of glass. Lane and Gabrielle snapped back against their seats and bounced yo-yo like between their seats and harnesses. Almost as if in slow motion, the plane settled back onto its tail. Silence reigned.

Gabrielle looked out. She realized that they had stopped. Then she looked at Lane. His head slumped forward. *Dear God in Heaven, is he dead?* She quickly released her harness and slid over to Lane. She said, "Lane, Lane are you okay?" In panic, she screamed, "Lane! Talk to me!"

Gabrielle Takes Charge

That moment, borne of desperation, Gabrielle metamorphosed unbelievably from a sophisticate to a survivor. Her acquired pomposity changed to an ardent pragmatism. She instantly developed a determination to live at all costs.

Calling on her First Aid training she put her left middle fingers against Lane's throat, feeling for his carotid pulse while she watched his chest for movement. She cupped her right hand over his nose and mouth, feeling for exhaled air. When she felt a pulse and saw his chest move, she joyously exclaimed, "Thank God. You're alive!"

She unbuckled his harness and only then noticed the blood on his shirt and lap. She lifted his head and labored to remove his helmet. Then she discovered the source of the blood. A two-inch gash ran across Lane's forehead, almost centered just above his eyebrows.

She thought, "If his helmet had extended to his eyebrows, he'd be okay." As she thought about Lane and their surviving the forced landing, she reached a wash cloth from her suitcase and placed it against his cut, applying direct pressure. Even though she tried to remain calm, she was terror stricken. Thoughts flashed through her mind:

What if Lane doesn't make it? What are my chances of getting out of this wilderness without him? Will we be found? Will we freeze? Oh, my God. What will I do?

Several minutes passed before Gabrielle removed the wash cloth to look at Lane's head. The bleeding had stopped. Just then Lane moaned.

Gabrielle said, "Lane, Lane. Are you okay?"

A mumbled response followed, "Uuhhh, uh, uhh. Where am I?"

"Lane, you're on the ground. We're okay. We came down after the engine quit. We're okay. We're on the ground," she soothed him.

He moaned, "Gab...Gabrielle...want...want water. Sooo t-h-i-r-s-t-y.”

Gabrielle, overwhelmed with excitement that he was conscious, joyously blurted, “Oh, Lane. You’re okay!” Though she questioned giving him liquid, Gabrielle retrieved a 7-up from the cooler, opened it and placed the rim to his lips, “Here, Lane.”

He drank thirstily. “Sooo good.”

Lane reached for the can and tried to chug its contents, but Gabrielle restrained him, “No, Lane. You shouldn’t drink too much.”

Just then he slumped forward. She grabbed him and kept him from hitting the instrument panel, then eased him back against the seat. She thought, “Oh, no. Now what?”

She was concerned about his head injury and knew the importance of monitoring it. Other than the head cut she assumed he had no open injuries.

Her efforts to awaken Lane were futile. She was relatively comfortable in spite of her inactivity, but for the first time she noticed the cold in the air. She looked at the thermometer on the top of the cabin. Ten degrees Fahrenheit. Then she discovered the hole in the windshield. She wondered how the hole got there and realized she must take action to retain as much heat as possible in the plane. Particles of glass covered the floor.

She thought of the emergency kit and scrambled from her seat. The first thing she did was to remove the cargo net behind the seats, realizing that without it the load would have hurtled forward and caused greater damage. She found the emergency kit. From it she took a flashlight, knowing she’d need it in the dark hours to come. Her Rolex read straight up noon.

She retrieved a utility knife from the tool box and stepped to a bale of furs. She cut through the burlap covering and pulled a fox pelt from the pile. Gabrielle then stuffed the pelt into the windscreen hole, effectively plugging it.

She went back to Lane, removed his mittens from his coat and slipped them over his hands. Then she struggled to get his coat on him. Her efforts were compounded by the size of the cockpit—less than 36-inches between the instrument panel and the seat back. She spoke to him, “Lane, I’m going to put your coat on. You need to stay warm. I’m going to take care of you. I’ll be right here until you wake up.”

Knowing that she couldn’t get his coveralls on him, Gabrielle could only hope he would regain consciousness and get them on later. She had a passing fantasy and almost laughed aloud when she thought about the best means of warming a hypothermic person—removing his clothes and going skin to skin.

She grabbed an armload of furs and dropped them on her seat. She arranged several around Lane’s legs up to his waist with the hair side on his clothes. She draped a couple of wolverine hides over his upper torso. In an effort to prevent his falling forward or dislodging the furs she used parachute cord from his survival gear bag to loosely tie Lane upright in his seat.

Gabrielle became a flurry of motion, knowing she must make preparations for surviving the night and maybe the days ahead, depending on what developed. She called upon her strength and independence.

She reached Kelly's coveralls. Gabrielle removed her coat and boots, then put on Kelly's coveralls and Sorels. Then she put her coat back on.

She opened more bales of furs and stacked some hides individually around the windscreen and between Lane and the door. After she stuffed furs between herself and her door, she arranged several around her legs and placed some over her upper body.

For the remainder of the afternoon she periodically tried to awaken Lane with no success, and she continued talking out loud for both his and her benefit.

In an effort to take her thoughts from the dilemma Gabrielle took out her diary.

Dear Diary,

What a difference a day makes! Yesterday I was fine. Today I'm fighting for my life. Something completely foreign has happened to me—I'm struggling harder to stay alive than I ever did in the Big Apple!

We've had a forced landing. My pilot is unconscious.

I'm hoping he has no internal injuries. Hopefully he only has a concussion and will regain consciousness soon.

Please, Lane, wake up. I need you so badly!

Time crawled. She couldn't stop looking at her watch every half hour, which turned out to be every four or five minutes! Although the river canyon now was in deep shadows, it was light for several hours before the sun set.

She thought about eating but couldn't bring herself to do it.

As darkness descended, she tried not to think of the hours ahead but rather focused on staying warm and taking things one step at a time. Before dropping off to sleep she thought, "Tomorrow will be a whole new day. We'll start fresh. I can't lose Lane like I did Gabe."

All night Gabrielle tossed and turned. Her current dilemma reminded her all too graphically of Gabe. If it wasn't the discomfort of sleeping upright and the reoccurring dreams of Gabe, it was the nightmares of the forced landing and Lane's condition.

Every time she awoke, she felt the flashlight in her gloved hands. She tossed the furs off and shone the flashlight on Lane, talked to him, assured herself that he was breathing and hoped he would come to. She noticed the gauze she'd taped to his forehead was still there and the blood on it was dry. A good sign.

In the darkness of early morning Gabrielle awakened. She felt a need to go to the bathroom, but she repressed that call of nature. At last a long night surrendered to a growing dawn. A sliver of silver silently slit the morning sky. Gabrielle was stiff and a little cold but alive. She now knew that she must answer that call of nature.

Tossing off her furs and removing the jammed hides from the doorway, she opened her door, slithered out the narrow opening and gingerly eased herself down the two tiny steps on the wheel strut. The 4-inch diameter metal pads were barely bigger than a can lid. It required a bit of balancing as she slipped from the first to the second one some fifteen inches lower. Then she stepped onto the tire.

She immediately noticed that the plane rested on a snow berm. It had skidded fifty feet up the beach from the river and ploughed a trail in the snow. This she followed to the tail end of the plane.

Complimenting herself for her thinking ahead when she had removed a roll of gauze from the emergency kit to use for toilet paper, she smiled. She could tell immediately that going to the bathroom on a wilderness river in the winter was more survival-oriented than jumping from bed nude in New York and using her apartment's fashionable plumbing. She wrestled her coat off, hung it over the elevator, struggled with her coveralls, then her pants. Finally she was down to bare skin. *Ohhhh, this is cold.*

Gabrielle climbed back into her seat and looked at Lane, buried beneath his furs. Unable to control herself any longer, she leaned over and kissed him on the lips. They were soft and warm. She thought of Marcus. Is it wrong to kiss Lane? Is kissing Lane more enjoyable than kissing Marcus? She'd like to find out if he were in condition to kiss her in return.

Then he groaned.

A surge of excitement coursed through her, "Oh, Lane. Lane? Are you awake?"

He groaned again and spoke slowly, "I'm not sure if...I'm awake... or dreaming. We're on the ground...on the river...and alive, right?"

"Yes." She asked, "Do you remember anything?"

"I remember dreaming that a thousand pound bundle of furs attacked me. I've never had a headache like this! How'd I get tied up?" He joked, "You didn't take advantage of me in my condition during the night did you? I have to go to the bathroom so bad. Would you mind stepping outside and going for me?"

Gabrielle lunged towards him and hugged him, "Oh, Lane. You're okay. I know you are because you're joking." She kissed him longer than she had earlier and didn't want to stop. "I've been so scared. I just couldn't imagine trying to survive this nightmare without you."

Lane replied, "Easy, easy. My head's killing me. You're an-altar-bound-woman. Besides I don't want your beau to find out that you've been kissing a perfect stranger. Heavy on perfect. It's hard telling what he might do to me. Now, if you can drag me out from under this man-eating fur pile, I'll see what I can do to rescue you. It's obvious you're a damsel in distress. But first I gotta go."

6

Inventory

While walking back to the cockpit from his bathroom stop Lane thanked God for delivering them from serious injury in the forced landing.

He wondered what caused the cut on his head, when he noticed broken pieces of glass on the ground. He looked up and noticed a dead spruce tree thrusting horizontally to the ground just in front of the propeller, spear like. The tip of the snag had splintered. Lane deduced that the plane, after striking the snow covered log, shot forward hitting the snag, causing the hole in the windscreen and stopping the plane's forward momentum and, consequently, smacking him in the head.

He told Gabrielle he was going to check out the plane and assess the surrounding area. She exited her passenger door and met him on the ground. They were roughly twenty yards from the river and 200 yards upstream from a huge pile of driftwood at the river's edge. Eons past the river had sliced through the country on its downstream journey creating a broad valley. The gradual hills to the east evolved into 4,000 to 5,000-foot high mountains. Seventy-foot tall cottonwoods lined the river. Thick brush patches pockmarked the banks. Back from the banks, spruce timber swept up-mountain to the 500-foot level where alder clumps clung to the steep sides with razor-edged peaks beyond. Lane noted the river's intermittent bare ice, patches of dirt and snow drifts covering the beach which bore mute witness to constant winds that he knew raked the area.

He felt confident that they would be rescued within a day or two. It wasn't terribly cold and probably wouldn't get more than twenty or thirty degrees below zero before spring's arrival.

Lane knew that flesh froze at 28 degrees Fahrenheit. He recalled some of his experiences in zero to minus 30 degree weather. He'd been warm in a quilted shirt and light polar fleece jacket with light cotton gloves and his wool hunting pants. His time outdoors taught him that cold was relative, depending on your experience with it and your state of dress. He felt comfortable knowing that they were well dressed and could keep a fire going day and night.

The still-intact plane would provide shelter and a bigger target for rescuers to spot. He would need to make sure the plane's top surface was kept snowless to provide contrast against the white of the snow for searchers.

Somehow when the plane bounced onto its nose the propeller was not damaged—at least it didn't appear to be. It shouldn't be a problem for the mechanic to troubleshoot it later. However with Gabrielle following him Lane examined the damaged wing and knew that even if he could find and fix the engine problem, coupled with the short landing area, he couldn't possibly fly *Tundra Bunny* out.

It was then that he noticed the faint odor of fuel. He checked the belly tanks and spotted a hairline crack in one. Wanting to reduce any danger of ignition, he decided to empty the fuel tanks.

In order to get to the horse trough, he removed the bundles of burlap bound hides, stacking them on the ground. Then he pulled the trough out, turned to Gabrielle and told her, "It's a good thing Bret sent this horse trough for my sister. It will be useful for a number of things. For starters, I'm going to drain the fuel from the belly tanks. There's a leak, and removing the fuel will lessen the danger when I build a fire.

"I'll use the fuel bucket to transfer fuel to the tub because the tub won't fit under the plane. I'll make a torch of dry wood behind the plane. If a plane shows up, we can touch it off as a signal fire."

He placed the fuel bucket beneath the rear fuel sump and pushed a screwdriver against the spring to allow fuel to flow, taking caution not to let it hit his hand. He knew that the fuel would be nearly the same temperature as the outside temperature, and, more importantly, that super cooled liquids freeze the skin.

Lane filled the bucket five times, each time transferring it into the tub. Then he dragged the tub twenty feet beyond the tail of the plane. He returned to the plane, took the Swede saw to a standing, dead snag nearby and dropped it. After cutting the snag into lengths he dragged each to the tub, formed a fire tipi and told Gabrielle, "I'll make a pile and douse it with fuel. The fuel will evaporate, but at least we'll have the fuel tank empty and a more burnable pile of wood. And maybe a torch if we see a plane."

He repeated the fuel-draining process several times before the three tanks were empty. Each time he hauled it to the pile and poured the fuel on until the entire pile had been doused a number of times.

Then Lane asked Gabrielle if she'd help him inventory the plane's contents. He told her, "I really got you into this. And after I told you a plane crash could ruin your day. I'm disappointed in myself. And I'm sorry, Gabrielle."

Gabrielle replied, "It's not your fault, Lane. Thank you for caring."

They climbed into the cargo hold. It was then that he discovered Gabrielle's handiwork of the night before. He looked at the fox tail sticking out of the window and said, "I understand that teenagers in the '50's and '60's hung dice and rabbit's feet from their car's rear-view mirrors. But I've never heard of a fox tail."

She knew him well enough by now to know he was kidding her.

Then he continued, "I'm sorry you have to endure this experience surrounded by animal skins."

Gabrielle responded, "Thank you, Lane. It's definitely not what I anticipated when I came to Alaska. We'll just make the most of it. I'm thankful we have this means of staying warm."

Lane said, "Well, if I don't miss my guess, we'll find several uses for the hides. The first thing we need to do is find out what we have in the way of food and survival gear. I want to call on the radio to see if we can raise anyone." He didn't tell her that because of the mountains, he wasn't too hopeful.

He turned on the radio and called another Mayday on one-two-one-five, giving their location. The only reply was the crackling of the radio.

He looked at the emergency locator transmitter and explained its function to Gabrielle. "A severe impact activates this transmitter. It can also be manually operated. About once an hour when a satellite passes over, it picks up the signal the transmitter emits. On the first pass it is recorded and on successive passes people can zero in on the location and send rescuers. If no signals are picked up after the first hit, the rescuers' job is compounded.

"Let's see what we have in the way of survival goodies." After examining the survival kit and checking the plane's compartments they accounted for:

> 1 large can of beef stew
> 1 large can of chicken noodle soup
> 1 dozen packets of Top Ramen noodles
> 1 dozen energy-protein bars
> 1 pint of coffee
> 1 Emergency Locator Transmitter
> 1 12 gauge flare gun and 6 flares
> 1 set of three Skyblazer flares
> miscellaneous ground signaling devices including a mirror
> 1 axe
> 1 Swede saw

1 tool kit
First aid kit containing steri strips, band aids, ankle wraps
          and ammonia capsules
1 flashlight
waterproof matches
2 sleeping bags
1 horse trough
a couple of dozen bales of animal furs
1 20x40 foot blue, poly tarp
1 cargo net
Lane's personal survival bag including:
his head lamp and extra batteries; magnesium stick; jerky; 5 packets of freeze dried food; Leatherman; parachute rope; space blanket; zip lock bag filled with packets of black tea, beef and chicken bullion powder; coffee; and First Aid kit.
Lane's .338 rifle and one box of 20 bullets;
Gabrielle's suitcase with her clothing and personal items;
Lane's hand bag containing personal items and an extra pair of underwear;
They each had coveralls, stocking caps and gloves or mittens.

Spotting a single roll of toilet paper in the emergency kit, Lane commented, "When it's gone, we'll have to resort to Mother Nature. Hopefully we'll be in Anchorage before that happens."

Gabrielle agreed, "I second that. We've also got the rest of the food your mother sent."

Lane said, "Why don't we eat? Then we can drag some wood up from the drift pile down the river and build a fire."

Then he changed the subject, "We can use the tarp as a windbreak. If the windbreak doesn't work to keep the wind away, we have other alternatives. If push comes to shove, we could make a frame and build a tipi which would hold in a great amount of the fire's heat. We'll see how it goes for a few days. We can attach the tarp to the inside wing to make a leanto. We'll layer furs on the floor of the cargo hold for insulation and store what we're not using under the tarp-tent, giving us more room in the plane to sleep.

"You can see that most of the ground around the plane is windblown with little snow. That's a plus because we won't have to fight the snow so much. I'm pretty happy that we lost the engine when we did. Had we gone into Shellabarger Pass, it would have been pretty nasty because of the big boulders and few places to sit down.

"If we need to move around in deep snow, I have Bret's snowshoes.

I can fabricate an extra pair if need be."

While they ate the last of the food from the cooler and shared a pop, a layer of ground fog crawled up the valley floor obliterating the mountains and reducing visibility to two hundred yards.

Lane exited the plane to get the tarp from a side compartment and saw the fog for the first time. He knew that would eliminate their chances of being seen.

Even though the Beaver was larger than the two place planes commonly seen in Alaska, it was still a small object to locate from the air. Her wings spanned 48-feet and she was just over 30-feet long.

He withdrew the tarp. Fashioning a piece of parachute cord between each corner of one end and tying a Crescent wrench to the center of the rope, he tossed the wrench over the left wing and pulled on the connecting rope, effectively pulling the tarp onto the wing. He then pulled the tarp over the wing, forming a tent with the wing as the ridge line. He anchored the ends of each side with two bales of furs.

Thinking it would get Gabrielle's mind off the dilemma and provide her some exercise, Lane said, "Let's take the saw and walk down the river to that pile of driftwood for some firewood." Even though it was foggy, he grabbed the flare gun. He wanted it with them in the event a plane flew over. Lane knew the Skyblazer flares had a 500-foot elevation and flashed 20,000 candle power, both greater than the flare gun; however the flare gun was easier to carry.

When Lane hadn't returned to AirLaska within his anticipated arrival time, his employer set the wheels in motion to begin a search. Searching for missing aircraft was nothing new in Alaska. Urgency ruled. But weather dictated the terms. AirLaska determined to send another pilot over Lane's route the first thing next day.

In the meantime Lane's boss acted. He knew Lane's record of prompt and consistent flight scheduling and was more than a little concerned. He knew established rescue procedure and called Kenai Flight Service—Kenai would check with other flight service stations around the state to see if they'd heard from or seen Lane's aircraft. If their response was negative, the search would be upgraded and they would notify the Rescue Coordination Center at Fort Richardson Army Guard near Anchorage.

Word got out. The Rescue Coordination Center spokesperson passed along the news, "Lane Morgan's down. He left Nulato with one passenger and a load of furs. Lane's top drawer. Few bush pilots are better. A high flier picked up a broken transmission. AirLaska reported him overdue but they haven't heard from him. We'll launch a full scale search tomorrow at 0700 hours."

RCC would try to assess Lane's flying habits, the amount of emergency gear on board and all available resources. Their findings would determine the urgency of the search. Normally the Civil Air

Patrol; the Alaska Air Guard; commercial jet liners, which monitor the emergency frequency, and private pilots took part. AirLaska volunteered all their aircraft for the search effort.

While RCC coordinated the search, leaders from CAP and the Air Guard checked their lists of support personnel and called them to see if they were available. Planes were readied. A ground support group was mustered—to prepare meals, to take care of lodging and to monitor the search activities.

Several circumstances called for various efforts—if no Emergency Locator Transmitter signals were received, pinpointing the plane's locale, a broader search area would result. The availability of aircraft dictated the size of the search. Search pilots normally flew a grid thirty minutes in one direction, 500-1000 feet above ground level, flying the grid in one mile parallel tracks. Sometimes the grid area was divided into four quarters with four pilots flying the same grid, in fifteen minute tracks.

Kenai Flight Service learned that a Mayday message had been received from a commercial jetliner but that the transmission was garbled. The Rescue Coordination Center initiated a full scale search.

While search efforts were organized, AirLaska contacted Lane's family, then called Gabrielle's mother in New York. They arranged with the rental company to pick up Gabrielle's rental car.

Lane's family knew enough about flying to assume a forced landing was probable. They also knew that Lane was capable of wilderness survival. They united in their hopes and prayers that Lane and Gabrielle were okay and that they would be rescued. Each recalled treasured memories of Lane.

Park volunteered to fly with the rescue effort. Loretta manned the phone, fielding calls from family and friends. She called Lane's boss and volunteered to be a liaison person for Gabrielle's family calls and to house the family should they choose to come to Alaska.

Two days later Gabrielle's mother and father arrived—Gwendolyn from New York and Dec from Denver. Park picked them up at Anchorage International Airport.

Even though they hadn't been together for years and it was difficult for Dec and Gwendolyn, Gwen said, "Hello, Dec. I'm so glad you're here. I knew you would come."

Dec replied, "We lost one child to the wilderness, but let's save this one. I'm going to do everything I can to bring her back alive. You can count on it."

They gathered their luggage from the baggage claim area and were off to the Morgans. When they arrived at Lane's, Loretta greeted them with open arms, "Gwendolyn and Dec, welcome to our home. We'll do whatever we can to make you comfortable."

Park and Loretta showed the Laceys their home and their designated sleeping areas and Park offered, "Feel free to make this home yours. The refrigerator, stove, phone and computer are at your disposal. If we can do anything to assist you, please let us know. No wish is too small.

"Let me assure you that Lane is abundantly skilled for his task. He's spent hundreds of hours in the outdoors and knows survival techniques. If any pilot can survive out there, he can."

Because of their long separation, it was only normal for Gabrielle's parents to remain distant from each other—Gwendolyn more so than Dec. They treated each other civilly at first and within a few days they became more amiable. Gwendolyn was concerned about Gabrielle's vegetarian diet and wondered what kinds of things were available in the plane. Even though they agreed that they didn't want to lose two kids to the outdoors, Park expressed that both children were doing what they loved when tragedy struck.

The Morgans and Laceys' parental love of lost children bound them; and they agreed to exhaust all energies toward finding their children.

Gabrielle and Lane encountered easy walking on the river ice near shore and in no time were at the drift pile. Most of the snow had been blown from the pile except in protected pockets. Lane began sawing through a forty foot log twelve inches in diameter. After a few minutes he stopped and removed his coat and coveralls telling Gabrielle, "As long as it's this warm, I can use the layer system to stay warm to keep from perspiring."

Lane cut one log into a two-foot section to be split for kindling with the axe at camp. He asked Gabrielle if she thought she could carry it. Next he cut four 8-foot lengths, secured one to his parachute cord and started dragging it up the ice toward their camp. Gabrielle carried his coat, coveralls and the short log.

Halfway to camp they heard the sound of a distant engine which grew louder and louder. Lane immediately pulled the flare gun from his waist band and checked to see that it was ready to fire. When the approaching airplane sounded to be within half a mile, he held the flare gun straight up and fired.

There was a pop followed by a swishing sound. Then the flare flamed to life, coloring the cloud bank overhead and dispersing red-orange smoke. Lane wasn't sure if the flare had emerged through the cloud layer making it visible to any pilot above, but he hoped it had.

They listened as the plane's engine reverberated through the fog 2000 feet overhead. Then the sound trailed off into silence.

In an effort to encourage Gabrielle Lane said, "They usually fly well past the rescuee before they turn around. When they've spotted someone, they usually circle or wiggle their wings from side to side."

Gabrielle's eyes widened as she asked, "But what if they don't come back?"

"It's okay," Lane said, "they'll keep on searching. At least we know they're looking for us. They'll find us."

The plane did not return.

When they reached camp, Lane placed the log on one end of the tarp between the two fur bundles anchoring it. He split kindling from the log that Gabrielle had carried. Then he placed the un-split block on the end of the tarp opposite the logged side.

Lane said, "I'll start a small fire. Our tent will capture some of the heat and keep the wind off. Lane removed the cigarette lighter he carried in case of emergencies and said, "While the fire gets started, I'm going to move enough furs from the cargo hold to make room for a sleeping area in the plane. I'm famished. Why don't we open a can of food to heat while I set the furs under the tarp?"

He asked Gabrielle if she'd like to start with stew or chicken noodle. As much as she hated the thought of eating meat, she chose stew, so he took the large can of beef stew, opened it with his GI can opener and set it by the fire.

Lane returned to the plane and moved all but three bales of furs under the tent. He stacked them in the shape of a couch six feet back from the fire, between it and the fuselage. Then he returned to the plane, opened the three bales and spread them out on the floor hair side up for insulation.

Lane asked Gabrielle if she'd mind opening his camp mess kit. She loosened the wing nut and removed the outside covers of the kit discerning that each was a bowl. Within were two plates, two cups and two plastic spoons. She smiled and asked, "So, what's with the two's? Is this your elopement China?"

Lane laughed, "No. I've had that mess kit forever. I take it everywhere I go with my survival gear. Usually, though, it's my mess kit for high mountain sheep hunts because it's light and adequate."

Gabrielle grinned again, held up his two plastic spoons and asked, "So, let me guess, these spoons were attacked by a ferocious campfire and you put out the flame before they were entirely consumed."

Pouring an equal amount of stew into each bowl he answered, "No. I'm always thinking of ways to lighten my pack, so I burned off the handles except for those stubs. You don't need a long handle; besides a long handle wouldn't fit into my mess kit."

Lane took the two cups and the empty stew can, filled them with snow and set them next to the fire to melt the snow.

As they ate, Gabrielle asked Lane how long he expected them to be there before rescuers showed up. He told her a couple of days and explained their situation, "We have everything going for us. First of all my boss expected us yesterday. There are only two reasons we wouldn't be there. The first is the weather. The second is a forced landing. We're close to a major flyway—people fly this route all the time. If they got our radio Mayday, they will be looking for us now, as that plane was probably doing. The ELT should have sent out a signal before it quit. So you can feel comfortable in the fact that we'll be okay."

Lane didn't tell Gabrielle that it was easy to lose an ELT signal as well as radio communication in this rough country.

"And another thing, we have enough food for a several days. If we're not rescued by then, we'll have to resort to something else for food. I can try for rabbits and ptarmigan or spruce hens. And there are moose around.

"I'm fairly well educated about edible plants. We'll see what we can find to supplement our food sources." Calling on his knowledge from past hunting trips in the surrounding mountains he said, "You can see this area's pretty windblown. It's normal. You can see lots of spruce and willow."

Gabrielle asked, "How can spruce and willow be used as food?"

"We can make spruce needle tea. We'll boil the spruce needles in water, flavoring it," Lane said. "The outer layer of young willow shoots can be peeled away and the inner section either scraped and added to liquid for a drink or eaten raw if tender enough.

"The main thing is to eat, stay warm and drink lots of liquids. Within a month or so the thaw will start. If worse comes to worst, we can float out of here on a raft. This river empties into the Kuskokwim where there are villages all along."

Gaining more confidence and comfort in their chances of survival, Gabrielle said, "You know, maybe this experience will be a photo essay opportunity for me. I'm going to take as many pictures of our experience as possible to record it for publication." She teased Lane with a theme, "I can write about the New York sophisticate who flies into the maw of Alaska's wilderness, crashes with a dashing young pilot and survives."

Lane jabbed back, "Yeah, your characters can be the Beauty and the Beast. And the Beauty rises from the ashes like the Phoenix."

She said, "Another angle would be to do something about my love of Alaska's beauty being challenged by a tragedy."

Lane teased, "Yeah. You can write about the awesome bush pilot and his air taxi service...drum up some business for my boss."

Thinking about fresh water Lane said, "On another subject if by chance we're here more than a few days, it would be nice to find a water source. Melting snow is a pain, and the river ice is so thick, it would be a real chore chopping through."

Thinking it would be good to show Gabrielle where they were and the difficulty of hiking out, he went to the plane, pulled out his aeronautical map, took it back to the couch and spread it out.

"Gabrielle, I want to show you where we are and some of the obstacles we'd have to contend with if we tried to hike out." Pointing to the map he said, "We're right here, you can see the contour lines between these two points. Those represent mountains. And these are glaciers. It would be nearly impossible to hike over these. However it may not be that difficult to follow the river out if it were windblown all the way. It's over fifty miles to civilization—further by the river.

"Two major problems present themselves: the weather and the fact that statistically our chances of rescue are better if we stay with the plane. We don't know what weather conditions will be like the next few weeks. We don't know how much snow there is in our pathway. We would be restricted in what we could take with us. It makes better sense to stay with the plane and await rescue.

"But just to be on the civilized side, I want to put together a toilet facility for centralization of sanitation and for your benefit. I'm going to find some suitable trees."

He walked up the beach to the edge of the timber and returned. "All I need is some rope, some furs and a little time. Would you help me?"

He reached into the plane for some of his parachute cord and an armful of furs, returned to the fire for Gabrielle and they walked back to the trees.

Lane said, "If you'll hold this limb, I'll tie it to both trees. We'll repeat the process with these other two limbs to form a triangle. Once we have the foundation of these three limbs we can form a lattice work of smaller ones to form a platform, cover them with fur and we have an outhouse. The only thing we'll need then will be sides, which we can make from other hides. We'll run three or four lines of cord around these three trees about two feet apart and overlap the hides starting at the bottom. That way it will be warmer using it and more private. What do you think?"

Gabrielle responded, "Is there anything you don't think of? And is there anything you can't do?"

He laughed, "It's all part of being an Alaska manly-man. That's what my brother-in-law Brad Risch calls real men." Then he added, "And another thing, my grandfather always said, 'If there's no one in the barn to milk the cow, you better do it yourself.' I've learned self-reliance."

Lane completed the lattice work then laid a soft, chocolate-colored beaver blanket (ed: term for hide) over the platform and cut a hole in the center running his knife blade along the wood as a gauge to complete the hole. He secured it on two sides and said, "Guess I'll have to pay for this hide."

Then he tied the three rows of cord around the trees, retrieved a bale of furs from under the tarp-tent and cut it open. Back at the tree he started at the bottom and placed the furs around the three sides, then overlapped two more rows upward. He finished the job by spreading two large wolverine furs over the top to form a roof. Then he secured them with cord.

He turned to Gabrielle and said, "Angel Eyes, we need more wood for the fire. In fact we might as well stockpile lots of wood just in case we get a big dump of snow or end up staying more than a few days. Do you mind helping?"

Gabrielle needed no time to consider his offer, but she didn't answer immediately because she was thinking about his nickname for her...I wonder if I should tell him why the name Angel Eyes has relevance? Then she said, "I'm not a total New Yorker, you know."

Then they walked to the drift pile again. It had warmed up to twenty degrees which was quite comfortable for Lane who wondered how it was affecting Gabrielle. "How are you handling the weather, Gabrielle?"

"I'm fine. Glad your sister loaned me her things. When she suggested I take some extra things and said that we'd be back in two days, I guess neither she nor I expected this. I'm okay."

Lane tied onto another section of the 8-foot log he'd cut and hauled it to camp, depositing it under the right wing. He explained to Gabrielle, "We can stack the wood here and transfer it over to the fire when need be. It's not necessary to cut the logs into smaller pieces. I can haul eight to ten foot chunks because it's dry driftwood; we'll let the fire be our wood chopper."

They returned to the drift pile, cut some more logs and left them for retrieval the next day. On the way back to the plane Lane dragged another. When they reached camp, he said, "Gabrielle, it's been a pretty full day. What say we drink something hot to warm up and to replenish our liquid loss, eat a few bites, then hit the sack?"

"That sounds good to me, Lane. You know, it's almost dark anyway. Without a light we could sit in the fire light and talk, but I vote for doing it tomorrow night. You know, I'm pretty bushed myself."

They melted snow in the two mess kit bowls and stew can until all were full of hot water. Lane poured Gabrielle some water. He added a packet of Top Ramen to the stew can while making tea. After they'd eaten, he filled the cups, bowls and can with snow to melt. Then he put on his best John Wayne imitation, "Well, Missy, here's to one good woman from one tuckered cowboy. Drink up, and let's head for the bunkhouse to bed down."

Gabrielle laughed. And she realized that he had just supplied her with his nickname, *from now on I'll call him Cowboy.* As they approached the cargo hold, Gabrielle couldn't help thinking about her past few days since arriving in Alaska. *Who would have ever believed it?*

Once inside Lane said, "There's plenty of room to be comfortable, almost as much as the cargo area of a Chevy Suburban—4-feet high, 4-feet wide and 8-feet long. Gabrielle, I know this is an unusual situation. In my family it's not customary for a man and woman to sleep together unless they're married. The main thing we need to do out here, like I said before, is to stay warm and get nutrition. It's not so cold that I couldn't sleep in the pilot's seat like I did last night. However it makes more sense for the two of us to bundle up together for warmth. We have the sleeping bags I always carry for emergencies, and we can cover those with furs. I promise I won't do anything inappropriate. Do you have any problem with those conditions?"

Gabrielle blushed, more from desire than from bashfulness, and said, "Lane, I've known you only two days. But in that time I've come to know you are a gentleman." Although she visualized a different form of sleeping with him and wondered if it might come to fruition, she said, "I wouldn't expect any improper behavior from you. I think it is wise to stay warm. No, I wouldn't have any problems sleeping with you."

They rolled out the sleeping bags.

Lane said, "I normally don't use a pillow, but you will probably want one to keep away from the furs." He rolled up his coat to form a pillow and placed it at the top of her sleeping bag.

As she loosened her clothing, Gabrielle replied, "Thank you, Lane."

Then he said, "I hope you won't mind my putting on my bed clothes. If you'll close your eyes momentarily, I'll slip out of my clothes and into my pajamas."

Gabrielle gasped, "You're kidding, right?"

Lane responded, "Would I kid you?" and he chuckled. "Even if I wore pajamas normally—which I don't, do you think I'd bring them on a trip like this? I hope you sleep well."

Lane and Gabrielle climbed into their bags fully clothed and pulled furs over themselves.

Gabrielle lay in her bag, evaluating the day's activities. She felt she was adapting to her situation and wondered if she would change much because of it. She thought *I'm already more aware of others' needs than before our forced landing. I know I'm talking and acting differently than before. It seems like I'm taking on some of the language and attitudes of those I've been around these past few days.*

She fell asleep thinking...*This is the first time I've ever gone to bed with so many clothes on. I wonder what it would be like to snuggle up next to Lane in my normal bedtime attire? What are my friends going to say when they find out I slept under all these hides? My life gets stranger by the day!*

47

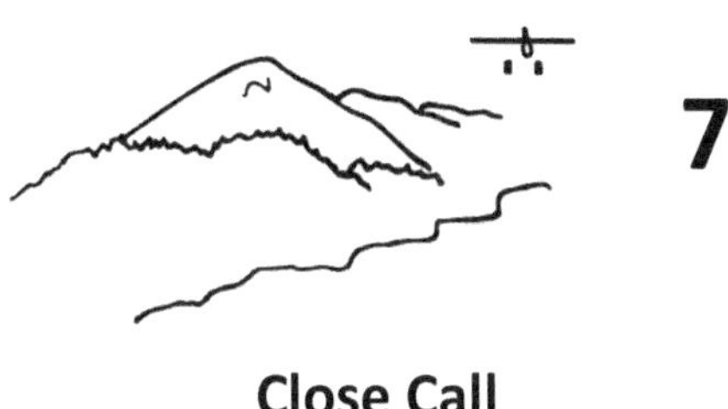

7

Close Call

Sunlight crept through the window the next morning and slowly crawled across the sleeping couple until it reached their eyes. Almost simultaneously they squinted, sat up and reached to cover their eyes from the sun.

Gabrielle turned to Lane, "You forgot to tell me before we went to bed that you snore," she complained, adding jokingly, "tonight I sleep outside."

"I'm sorry. I did forget to tell you," Lane admitted, "but I usually snore only when I'm super-tired. Give me a second chance, huh?"

"Okay," she said, "one last chance."

They left their sleeping bags and slid out the cargo door onto the ground.

Pearly white peaks poked proud heads skyward in sharp contrast to the sky's pale blue. Snow crystals glistened in the sunlight, a carpet of yellow-white gold showcasing the mother lode of beauty. Sunlight pierced the trees across the river, casting a brown-orange hue to the willows and a light purple to pockets of leafless trees on the hill beyond. Not a breath of air stirred as the cold, chill fingers of frost stabbed sharply like sabers.

Lane knew from experience that the temperature hovered around twenty below. He said, "If you want to use the bathroom first, I'll build up the fire."

After Gabrielle disappeared, Lane stirred the coals, tipied some kindling, blew on the coals and watched the wood catch fire. Then he filled their containers with snow so it would start melting while he took their can of chicken and noodles, opened it and set it by the fire. Next he returned to the plane and tried the radio. The only response was an endless, unnerving crackling. Lane split a piece of kindling from the short log to use as a stir stick for the noodles.

Gabrielle returned and made straight for the fire to warm up, then went to the airplane. When she emerged, it was obvious she'd had an encounter with her hair brush.

They stood by the fire warming the chill from their bones and nursing movement back into their bodies. Blue-white smoke tendrils squirreled slowly into the clear air, curling and wafting from side to side and periodically stalking them. They switched from one spot to another trying to stay warm close to the fire while avoiding stinging eyes and coughing from the smoke.

Warming up somewhat Gabrielle approached Lane and said, "Let me get a look at that cut on your head." He leaned forward a bit and she carefully examined his injury. Then she said, "It looks good. I can't see any foreign matter and it's starting to scab over. It looks like it's healing nicely. I think it's time to apply a butterfly band-aid or two."

Lane agreed then, realizing that he had forgotten to consider her feminine needs, said, "If there's anything I can do or something comes up and you need my help, please feel free to let me know."

Thankful for Lane's consideration she responded, "That's thoughtful of you Lane. Thank you."

After Gabrielle "doctored" Lane's head, he suggested they eat breakfast and go for a walk upriver for the exercise. He wanted to look for some branches to fabricate an extra pair of snowshoes. Lane carried the saw and his snowshoes in the event he would need them to walk over any deep snow to a tree should he find the required limbs.

By the time they left camp, a chilly, gray-white fog blanket obliterated the sun. Knowing the best time to be rescued is within a few days after a forced landing Lane hid his disappointment in the weather's change for the worse. Nevertheless he carried the flare gun in his waist band.

As they trudged over the river ice, avoiding deep snow drifts, they joked and laughed, enjoying each other's company.

Lane pointed out a snow covered hump stretching across a backwater slough and said, "Beneath that snow is a dam the beavers constructed. That seven foot mound in the center of the slough is the beavers' house, often referred to as a lodge." He chose not to mention it, but figured he could remove the snow and the top of the house to utilize the occupants as a food source later if necessary.

As they continued, Lane constantly scanned the nearby trees for suitable snowshoe wood. Quarter mile upstream he stopped abruptly and pointed to the brush lined bank another thirty yards beyond. He said, "There's a stream mouth ahead entering the river." He knew that any water in the area, whether river, pond or lake, would normally be frozen to a depth of at least two feet. But he was also aware that warm springs stay open year around. "Maybe we'll have drinking water." He hurried ahead, turned to his right, mounted the low bank and turned excitedly to call to Gabrielle.

He didn't realize she was right behind him and nearly knocked her down when he turned. "Gabrielle, there's open water. See the fog-like vapor. That indicates open water. There must be a warm spring in the stream. We can get water here without melting snow."

Gabrielle shared his joy, "That's great, Lane. It will save us time and work."

He responded, "I'm not sure about the work, because we'll have to haul it to camp. But it will definitely save melting time."

They continued upriver. Spotting a likely tree, Lane stopped and said, "I think I can use those limbs for the snowshoe frame. Why don't you wait here. I'll put on Bret's snowshoes and cut the limbs in a jiffy." Even though he felt the fog would hinder passing pilots from seeing them, Lane said, "Then we should probably head back. I don't want to get too far away from camp in case the fog clears and a plane comes by. We'll need to torch our signal pile."

He donned the snowshoes, hurried to the tree, cut the limbs and turned to retrace his steps. From his vantage point above the river ice he noticed tracks beyond Gabrielle. He carried the saw and limbs back, set them down by Gabrielle and told her, "I saw some tracks just beyond you. I'll check them out and be right back."

When Lane reached the tracks sixty yards beyond Gabrielle, he was shocked to realize they were made by a grizzly. But more surprisingly they were made within the last twenty-four hours.

He hurried back to Gabrielle. While removing his snowshoes he told her it was important for them to get to camp right away, "We'll need my rifle. There's a winter grizzly sashaying around here and something's got to be wrong with it. It's too cold and there's too much snow for a bear to be out at this time of year. Let's go."

They'd gone a dozen yards when they heard a rumbling sound. They froze in their tracks, listening intently. The sound grew louder, and closer. Suddenly they recognized the sound as that of an airplane.

They looked at each other and simultaneously shouted, "Airplane!" Lane pulled the flare gun from his waist band and prepared to fire as the plane got closer. Lane told Gabrielle," I don't think they'll see the flare. The fog layer probably extends beyond the flare's trajectory. I think the plane's higher than yesterday. Either the weather's worse up there, forcing them above the ridge or they may be commercial and on a commute." At length he chose not to fire the flare gun. From the sound he knew the plane passed over a mile above them.

While they quickly walked the few hundred yards to camp, Lane constantly swiveled his head looking for the owner of the bear tracks. They reached camp and Lane asked Gabrielle to take the saw and limbs under the tarp while he got his rifle. He dragged a log onto the fire to maintain its heat output.

When he approached Gabrielle, he told her that they should keep the rifle with them at all times in case the bear showed up. Respecting her disdain for firearms he didn't wish to cause her further grief. But he felt it was necessary for their safety that she know about the rifle and its proper functions. He showed her the procedure of loading and aiming, telling her, "If for some reason I'm not with you and you need to fire it, this instruction should help."

They kept a watch for the bear, but it never showed.

Lane asked Gabrielle if she was familiar with freeze dried food.

"Yes, I've eaten some. Do you want me to prepare a meal while you work on the snowshoes?"

Lane thought that was a good idea. He started working on the snowshoe frames while Gabrielle melted snow for water.

After they ate, Gabrielle said she thought she would take a nap on the fur couch. She felt it was warm enough under the tarp to keep her from getting too cold. Lane told her he'd finish the snowshoes and when she woke up he'd haul more firewood.

It seemed like only moments, but it was an hour later that Gabrielle awoke. Lane looked at her and smiled, "Why, Gabrielle, how disheveled your hair looks this fine day."

With impish glee she responded, "The better to scare you with."

Lane realized it had been a few days since they'd had a chance to clean up. He suggested they use the horse trough for a bath tub. Lane told Gabrielle he could clean it with the aid of the plane's fuel bucket. Although it was virtually a brand new galvanized tub, four feet long, two feet wide and two feet deep, he figured he could melt enough snow for enough water for Gabrielle to bathe.

Lane went to the plane and retrieved the bucket that he had used to drain the fuel tanks. He removed the chamois covering the mouth and filled the bucket with snow then placed it by the fire.

Then he told Gabrielle, "I'm going to scour the bucket then the tub. Then I'll put the tub in the plane and fill it with hot water. I'll keep myself occupied cutting wood until you've had a chance to bathe in private. What do you think?"

Gabrielle was overjoyed with the idea and said, "How long do you think it will take to fill the tub?"

"It would be safer for both of us if you accompany me with the rifle to the spring. May take several trips. We haul water back, heat it and fill the tub. Mind you, when I say 'fill,' I don't mean to the top. While water's heating, I'll level the tub with driftwood then cover the tub with hides to hold in enough heat until there's enough water for your bath."

"They walked to the spring and returned, alert for the grizzly. When the first bucket warmed, Lane leveled the tub. On the second return and while water heated, he insulated the tub by furs around it. When he'd brought the twelfth bucket to the plane, he set a fur over the bucket and told Gabrielle, "This last one is pretty hot. I'll set it on these two logs on the floor and you can add it if your water gets too cold. In the meantime I'm going to the woodpile. You're good to go. When you're done, give a holler, and I'll come back.

"Be careful not to get too much water on the floor or it will freeze and melt while we're sleeping on it, getting us wet and cold. I have an extra flannel shirt in my gear if you want to use it for a towel. I can dry it later. I'm going to leave the rifle by the door. I'll keep an eye out for the bear. If I see it, I may join you. I'll take the flare gun. Some old timers swear by flares as bear stoppers. You going to be okay?"

"I can't think of any reason I won't." She joked, "Can I trust you to go to the wood pile, or are you using cutting wood as a ruse so you can sneak back and watch me?"

"In your dreams, Angel Eyes," he retorted. Lane took the saw and started for the drift pile, "I'm outta here."

As he walked, the fog layer continued to lift, hovering a thousand feet above. He noted a slight breeze blowing at his back, almost as if it were following him down river. Visibility was unimpaired below the cloud. He thought about their need for food, knowing that freeze dried nourishment would be gone in another day. They could survive a while on his bouillon, tea and coffee, but he knew they needed solid food. He didn't want to alarm Gabrielle by raising the subject of killing something to eat. Nevertheless he knew their survival depended upon it.

Meanwhile Gabrielle entered the cargo hold and, because of the cold, she removed her layers of clothes quickly. She maneuvered around the bucket of hot water on the logs and peeked out the window to see where Lane was. Then she removed the hides from the top of the tub and tested the water for warmth before stepping into it. Although it was only half dozen inches deep, she sat down, delighting in the water's warmth.

She instantly savored the pleasure of getting clean. As Gabrielle basked in her new found luxury, she hummed and compared this strange bath to others she'd taken under much better conditions. She hurried to avoid the cold beyond the water, occasionally looking out the window and enjoying the surrounding beauty and Lane's activity.

She watched him saw and stack wood next to the drift pile and realized how thorough and efficient he was. His stamina and power did not escape her attention either.

She washed and rinsed her hair. While washing it the second time she thought about the many times her father complimented her when growing up. He had always loved her hair and told her how beautiful it was. The hair that normally hung half dozen inches below her shoulders was a soapy, soppy gob of thickness in her hands. She rinsed it thinking that it was about as clean as it could get under the circumstances.

Unaware that the grizzly whose tracks they'd seen was that very moment in the vicinity, Lane and Gabrielle pursued their separate activities. The grizzly foraged the surrounding forest for sustenance. A grizzly will eat anything it can get hold of—everything from berries to carrion. A few maverick grizzlies have killed humans for food.

As it ambled near the river through and around patches of brush in varying snow depths, it searched for anything edible. The bear dug unsuccessfully at rabbit holes. It ripped at rotten logs and chomped on grubs. It relied almost entirely on its nose for the grizzly lives and dies by its powerful olfactory sense.

In the midst of ripping at another log the animal stopped abruptly. Instantly, it stood erect on hind legs and pointed its rubbery black nose skyward in the direction of the river.

The scent assailing his nostrils plastered images in his conditioned brain, images of campfires. And man's food. This bear had lived a long life and fought many battles with sows he sought to mate and boars competing for the sow's ardor. He'd stolen into campsites at night to raid coolers and food supplies. Now the compelling aroma on the wind riveted his attention. Man smell. Warm food smell.

In a half-lope, the big boar plowed through the snow to the river's edge. He stopped and rose on hind legs again, testing the wind. Across the river he spotted a moving figure. Food.

The grizzly started its stalk, utilizing every bit of cover between it and the man-food target.

First the bear crept behind a snowdrift. As it narrowed the gap, the bear dropped to its belly, extending its front paws like a giant cat. Then it belly-crawled toward the unsuspecting wood-cutting man. Slowly. Methodically.

All but finished rinsing her hair and daydreaming, Gabrielle pictured her past few days. She verbalized her thoughts, "Some flight seeing trip." Then she laughed at herself for making the comment out loud. She was about to step from the tub's warmth and cleansing balm to towel off and dress when she looked out the window.

Gabrielle thought she saw a dark object on the river. Peering more closely, she realized it <u>was</u> something. A bear! She knew immediately that this was the bear Lane had talked about. As she lunged from the bath, Gabrielle caught a fleeting glimpse of its stalking movement. *It's crawling toward Lane just like a big cat.*

She didn't have time to think, only to react. She tossed on her parka without zipping it. She snatched the rifle from its resting place, jumped into her boots and scrambled from the plane. Gabrielle threw herself across the tail of the Beaver and aimed at the bear. By this time its stalk had brought it to within thirty yards of Lane.

The next thing she knew, she heard an explosive report, felt a jar and heard a thundering echo across the valley floor, reverberating back to her off the mountainsides.

At the crack of the rifle, the grizzly bellowed a blood curdling roar of defiance, a death defying blast that all but shook the earth. Almost before it was down, the brown hulk shot up off the ice, spun around and bit at its shoulder. The emaciated beast stopped and looked in a questioning manner toward the Beaver. Then it turned slowly to face Lane, momentarily staring at the man-thing.

Almost quicker than the eye can record Gabrielle chambered another round and fired a second shot.

Looking up from the recoil of the .338, Gabrielle saw the bear down and motionless. Then she saw Lane running toward her. She heard him hollering but couldn't make out his words.

It was then that she realized she was nearly naked, and she reacted accordingly. She ran quickly under the tarp, leaned the rifle against the couch and zipped up her parka. Just then Lane ran up to her.

He threw his arms around her, drew her to his barrel chest and shouted, "Are you okay?"

By now she was shaking, "Y-y-yes. I c-c-can't believe w-w-hat just happened. I t-t-think I'm going to f-f-faint."

Although shaken, Lane was concerned about her and wanted to get her mind off the event. He teased her, "I don't think it would be wise to faint in your condition of dress. I'm only human, ya know. "

Then he mimicked her, "You know, since you've got little glaciers forming on your knees, let's get you over by the fire to warm you up. That's got to be the most exciting bath you'll ever take!"

He led her to the fire and commented, "I don't know what you're wearing under that coat, but I have a feeling it's a good thing it's three-quarter length."

Gabrielle said, "Oh, Lane. I'm so glad you're okay. I just can't believe I did what I just did."

Realizing Gabrielle had quit shaking and appeared to be warming up, he asked, "Getting warm?"

Gabrielle replied, "Yes."

Lane said, "Let me get your clothes. While you're warming and dressing, I'll go check the bear. I want to make sure it's dead and unable to come after us. Call me when you're finished, and I'll come back. Okay?"

He grabbed her suitcase, carried it out to the couch and asked, "Are you okay?"

Gabrielle answered, "Yes. I'll be fine. Thank you."

Lane picked up the .338 and left.

When Lane reached the bear, he noticed two bloody areas soaking into the snow. One was near its left shoulder; the other was under its head. He immediately wondered how a person who deplored killing could take up a rifle and make a hundred and seventy yard shot to kill a grizzly in its tracks. It baffled him; but he determined to find out as soon as he talked with Gabrielle again.

The bear was extremely thin. Lane noticed a crooked jaw and a number of porcupine quills in its face with festering injuries, puss extruding at the quill roots. He realized this was a very hungry, very desperate animal.

While examining the bear and thinking, he heard a muffled shout and turned toward the plane. There stood Gabrielle fully clothed waving at him. He turned from the bear and walked toward the aircraft.

Approaching Gabrielle he asked, "Are you doing better now?"

She said, "I think so. I'm still processing it."

He told her he wanted to talk about it but first wanted to prepare some snow water. He walked to the fire, picked up a can, filled it with snow and set it by the fire.

Then he said, "Gabrielle, you said you deplore killing. You are an animal rights advocate. If that is so, how were you able to do what you just did with my rifle?"

8

Revelations

A pained look came over her face, "When I saw that bear stalking you, something snapped in me. I don't know if it was fear for your safety, fear for our saftey or what, but I automatically responded. I willed your safety. I instinctively fired the rifle at what I knew to be a lethal point..."

Lane interrupted her, "But how did you know about a lethal point if you deplore hunting? Do you know you broke the bear's shoulder? Then as it rose on three legs, you blew its brains out."

Gabrielle explained her position, "You know, I grew up with firearms. My father taught me to shoot. I've hunted extensively."

Momentarily surprised, Lane stood listening intently…absolutely amazed by her words.

She continued, "We hunted pheasants, waterfowl, deer and elk. I was pretty good at it, if I do say so myself. My dad hunted ducks so much that his friends nicknamed him Dec, for decoys."

Shocked, Lane asked, "You've hunted?"

"Yes. One day I was duck hunting at my father's club when there was an accident. The facts of the situation are that the safety on the twelve gauge was defective. My father and my twin brother..."

Visibly surprised, Lane interrupted again, "Your twin brother! You have a brother?"

"Had." Gabrielle's voice cracked.

Lane noticed her eyes were getting moist. Compassionately, he put his arm around her shoulders, and she continued haltingly, "My father and...brother were...in a duck pit across the lake...from my uncle and me. A flock of mallards whistled over. Dad gave the feeding call, and the green heads set their wings over dad's decoys. All of a sudden... there was...a...blast.

"My uncle and I looked at each other wondering what had

happened because the ducks weren't in range when the shot rang out.

"Then we heard a shout. 'Help! Quick, I need you!' my father screamed. We rowed our boat across the pond and discovered that Gabe," her comments continued slowly, "...had...been...shot.

"Dad was frantic. He wanted to get Gabe to the hospital as quickly as possible. While I followed behind, dad and my uncle carried Gabe to the van a few hundred yards away at the duck shack. Dad and I took off while my uncle called 911 and told them where the ambulance could intercept us.

"We met the ambulance a few miles away and rushed Gabe to medical help." Taking a slow, deep breath she continued, "But Gabe, he...a...he...didn't...make it. That was the turning point in my family's life..."

Sensing Gabrielle's anguish, Lane drew her closer and said, "I'm very sorry, Gabrielle. It must have been very difficult for you and your family over the years. Maybe we can talk about it later."

"Yes," she replied, "very hard. Seeing that bear sneaking towards you brought everything back. That's the reason I said, 'I can't believe what I've just done.' It was amazing to think that I picked up the rifle, that I recalled the sequence involving the safety, aiming, re-loading and so on."

Lane said, "In light of your tragic loss, I'm amazed you could ever handle a firearm again." But," Lane admitted, "I'm mighty glad you did! That bear could have ruined my whole year! It wasn't more than thirty yards from me when I heard the shot and turned. I hadn't seen it. I don't know if you know it or not, but a running grizzly can cover thirty yards in two to three bounds...in less than two seconds. It would have been on me before I could have used the flare gun. I owe you my life."

Gabrielle smiled and said, "So far that makes us even."

Lane queried, "How are you feeling now? Want to rest?"

"I'm fine," she replied. "I'm even willing to help you with that bear. Maybe we could use it for food."

Surprised by her consideration of eating the bear, Lane said, "Good idea. The Department of Fish and Game requires anyone killing a bear in defense of life and property to fill out paperwork to justify his action. Technically we're supposed to take the skull and hide to them. If you want to help me skin the bear, that would be great. We can salvage the meat and try to eat it; but I'm wondering how edible it would be considering the bear's condition."

They walked to the drift pile to retrieve the axe then headed to the bear. Lane showed Gabrielle the animal's claws and teeth, taking special care to point out the festered flesh. He said, "This beast was starving. See how skinny it is? It must have suffered great pain in its quest for survival.

"See this long scar along the side? It looks like a bullet wound; I suppose it could even be from a broadhead. Pity the person who shot this bear if the bear attacked him." Lane pointed out other scars, including a missing left ear, and told Gabrielle they were probably caused from fights with other bears or possibly with moose.

As soon as Lane peeled back part of the hide and exposed the carcass, he realized they could not eat it. He pointed out the greenish-yellow cast to the meat and told Gabrielle, "If we absolutely have to, we'll eat this bear. But I'm afraid we'll get sick if we try."

Gabrielle asked if he was sure. She was still questioning killing animals and hoped it wouldn't be necessary.

Gabrielle jockeyed herself around the animal as Lane requested her to hold different legs. Lane skinned the bear up to the ears then chopped through the neck with the axe. At length Lane flopped the head onto the hide, grabbed the bear skin by the shoulders and dragged it hair side down back to the plane.

He told Gabrielle, "I'll lay this hide out on the snow. It will freeze. Maybe we can use it then for something, like a wind break."

Lane stoked the fire with a log and said he would go to the spring for a bucket of water. "When I get back, we can wash our hands, clean up, cook another meal of freeze dried food and drink something hot."

Looking up at him from the couch Gabrielle said, "I'd like to go with."

Lane smiled, reached out a hand and helped her to her feet, "Okay, Angel Eyes," he teased, "I'll carry the bucket to the spring, and you can carry it back."

He turned to leave, and she jumped on his back, "No way, Cowboy, you can carry me there, and I'll carry the water back."

When they returned from the spring with the pail of water, Lane set it by the fire to warm, then he and Gabrielle sat on the edge of the couch.

Lane decided to tell Gabrielle Alaska's classic bear story. "This bear is like the bear called Old Groaner, probably Alaska's best known bear story. The tale goes a long way to portraying the maligning of a truly majestic animal. Old Groaner was injured by man before the bear became a renegade.

"Two Johnstone brothers prospected the Unuk River near Ketchikan in the 1930s. One dark night as they sat next to their camp fire, Bruce's dog Slasher snarled at something in the blackness beyond their fire ring. They looked up in time to see a dark hulk disappear into the ebony, groaning a mournful moan. Needless to say they slept little that night.

"The next morning they discovered large brown bear tracks just beyond reach of the fire's light. For several years they traveled the upper reaches of the Unuk and heard that mournful moan many times. They nicknamed the bear Old Groaner.

"Everything came to a head one day when Bruce was on the river bank with his dog and the bear lunged past him. Slasher hurtled through space at the charging bear which came out of nowhere. Bruce grabbed and fired his rifle just as the beast reached him, killing it.

"Bruce examined the bear's hide and found it hairless and very tough. The bear had five bullets in its skull—its right side was shot away. Its cheekbone was destroyed. Its unhealed jaw hinge was shattered and its fangs were growing grotesquely to one side. The animal's teeth were decayed and broken. The bullets were in the underside of the bear's skull and in all probability belonged to a trapper who had vanished on the river twelve years before—he had carried two weapons whose bullets were the same calibers as those found in the bear."

Gabrielle said, "That's both amazing and sad. To think that the man died and that the animal suffered for so long. How many bears are like Old Groaner and this one?"

"Very few. A bear that attacks a man is very rare. Bears maul only a few people a year in Alaska. On a related subject, however, figuratively speaking it's interesting to think that we each have a bear in our lives, something that stalks us or provides some obstacle for us."

"That's an interesting concept, Lane. I'll have to think about that. You know, it's really incredible how man and animal have co-existed for so long."

"Yes, it is. In many ways both are dependent upon each other. All human life is sacred, imbued with the command of God: 'let there be life'. He didn't say, 'Let there be death.' It is incumbent upon man to utilize what God has provided in a grateful manner—to ignore God's goodness and His plan is to desecrate it. To hallow His name and plan demands our respect for Him and obedience to it. We can do no less."

More and more Gabrielle grasped the importance of Lane's convictions and his common sense. She acknowledged the savagery of the wilderness as reality and questioned her ideals about saving the animals. She realized that as part of the food chain, she was a nutrient much the same as a carrot. A new awareness overcame her...that as a thinking creature with a soul, her life was more significant than the lives of animals.

Gabrielle agreed, "Coming to Alaska and seeing the struggle for survival has kindled some thinking. It's amazing that the bear I shot and Old Groaner were both abnormal bears. It's interesting to note that both animals charged man and were killed by a rifle. I'm reminded of my father's teaching that a rifle can yield good or bad results depending on whose hands it's in."

"Sounds like your dad has a lot going for him. I agree with him. Where man lives off the land or must defend himself against its inhabitants—be they animal or human—a firearm has distinct advantages. Firearms are a tool in much the same way as a carpenter's nail apron, a cowboy's saddle or a software wizard's computer. We all use tools in our every day professions. You use a camera; I use a plane. Both are essential to us.

"Equally important as the tool is the knowledge of how to use it. Ignorance renders the best tool useless. The rifle is only one tool used by Alaskan outdoorsmen.

"Because Alaska's extremes are shared by no other state—bigger mountains, colder waters and more diverse geography, Alaska demands more of her inhabitants. When you enter her wilderness, you must be prepared to battle the savagery she slings at you, be it surging seas, frightening forests, monstrous mountains or gaping glaciers. She requires more for survival. She's as wild as the wolves her wilderness whelps. Alaskans and newcomers must learn to adapt to her ways or perish.

"Alaska's ruggedness is characterized by the animals and people that inhabit her. She engenders a spirit of kill or be killed as well as a spirit of self-reliance and freedom.

"That pretty much brings us to the present. We're down to decision time. We have plenty of water, a good shelter and fuel supply. What we need now is a food source. We're not going to eat each other...

Gabrielle interrupted, "You mean like those South American soccer players who crashed in the Andes Mountains a few decades past...the ones who resorted to cannibalism?"

"Yes, those and others. Cannibalism was unfortunate but necessary.

"We often engage in decisions and activities—some unpleasant—necessary for survival. Sometimes the hunter-gatherer mentality should not only be tolerated but embraced. Hunter-gatherers chose to live."

Realizing that her survival depended upon obtaining food, very likely in the form of meat, Gabrielle replied without hesitation, "I choose to live."

To Kill or Not to Kill

Lane determined to make snares to catch rabbits. Rummaging through their survival gear for snare-making materials, he found a roll of wire in the tool box and fashioned a dozen circular frame snares.

Respecting Gabrielle's dislike of killing, he told her he'd go out alone. She told him she'd like to go along.

They gathered the snares, Bret's snowshoes and the crude pair Lane had made, his rifle and the water bucket before leaving the campfire. As they walked, Lane explained that he might be able to find ptarmigan.

Gabrielle queried, "I know they're the state bird; but they're not very big are they?"

"They're about the size of a pigeon. They often stay under snow covered clumps of grass to get out of the cold. The snow provides an insulation cover for them. You watch for ptarmigan tracks leading into a snow hump. Then you sneak up on it, cup your hands and reach into the snow to catch the bird."

Gabrielle wasn't sure whether he was kidding or not but after asking him she concluded that he was serious.

He also told her to keep her eyes peeled for moose, "If we get a moose, we'll have nutrition forever. Meat from a moose can feed a family of four for a year." He reminded her of the importance of fluids to keep from dehydrating and to promote proper bodily functions. "We don't have vegetables, but it's not likely we'll get scurvy. We won't be here that long. We can look for some Labrador tea bushes. That will help. And we can make spruce needle tea. There's an outside chance we might even find some rose hips."

Though Gabrielle had some experience with the outdoors and survival training, most of what Lane talked about was new to her. She listened with the growing realization that living off the land was possible, especially given the time to prepare properly.

Lane pointed out rabbit trails to her and they spent a couple of hours setting the snares. They stopped at the spring on their return to camp and Lane filled the water pail with icy, clear water.

Back at camp Lane set the bucket by the fire to heat water. He told Gabrielle, "We should have at least one rabbit in our snares by tomorrow. I'll check them first thing."

During the night Lane awakened and noticed a reddish glow through the windscreen. "Hmmm," he thought, "think I'll wake Gabrielle to show her." He gently ran his finger tips across her lips. She pursed and puckered her lips a couple of times to the tickling sensation. Lane suppressed laughter and continued. He cooed, "Wake up, Sleepy Head. Sleepy Head, wake up."

Finally Gabrielle rubbed her lips with her right hand. She opened her eyes and looked toward Lane. When her eyes adjusted to the dark, she realized that he was kneeling beside her. Somewhat concerned for being awakened in the middle of the night, Gabrielle questioned, "Lane, is something wrong?"

"I've got a surprise for you. It's an aurora alert."

"A what?"

"An aurora alert. My family and a few friends call each other to let them know when we see the northern lights. So they can enjoy them too. Sometimes we get calls at one in the morning."

Rubbing her eyes Gabrielle groaned, "What kind of joke are you pulling now, Lane?"

"No joke, Angel Eyes. Can you scoot out of your bag to your knees?" He placed his hands over her eyes and said, "Let me turn your head. When I say 'open,' I'll remove my hands and you'll be in for a thrill."

Turning her head toward the glow he said, "Open."

Shades of red spread across the vast canopy of space. Pulsating fingers of colors, varying from red to florescent green, intensified in both breadth and brilliance as they blazed upward thousands of feet before trailing off in rainbow arcs, flowing like banners blowing in the breeze. Like a herd of wild-eyed broncos, nostrils flaring and sides heaving, carrying men onto the battlefield in a galloping cavalry charge—   guidons rattling, bugles blaring, guns spitting lead and sabers slashing—the bright rose fingers swept in waves above the naked snow...only to retreat, regroup then charge again...and again... and again.

Gabrielle gushed, "Oh, Lane. They're so incredibly beautiful."

"Yes, they are. Every time they're different. Those myriad fingers glide like a pianist's hands, frequently accompanied by a hissing, crackling sound. The fingers bend and dance back and forth over the keys of a baby grand, ever probing the purple-black of the keyboard sky."

For several minutes they gazed in awe with renewed appreciation for the raw, natural beauty around them. Then they crawled back into their sleeping bags and went to sleep.

The next morning Lane's first activity was trying the radio. He called several "Maydays" with no response. Then he took his snowshoes and started off to check the snares while Gabrielle busied herself with her personal grooming.

Lane found no rabbits until he reached their third set. It held a plump snowshoe hare. He hung it in the notch of an alder and continued on until he'd checked every snare, resetting the ones which held rabbits. There were three hares total. On his return to camp he collected each.

He cleaned and skinned each rabbit and set them in the snow away from the fire. He then walked a short way from camp, cut green limbs and returned to build a roasting rack of driftwood and the green limbs. Then he placed the rabbits on the rack above the flames where they were soon simmering.

Lane told Gabrielle, "We'll ration our food, just in case we run into some blank days or run out of rabbits. I'm going to haul some wood to replenish our supply. Would you keep an eye on the cooking?"

"Certainly, Lane. I'll do my best."

"If you need me, holler. " As an after thought he teased, "Or jump into your bikini, and I'll come running."

The afternoon passed quickly, and before they knew it, darkness was upon them. The couple observed their nightly ritual of a tea warm-up. Then they steeled themselves away in the cargo hold under their fur insulation and, hoping for rescue the next day, went to sleep.

At daylight they resumed their routine morning activities which consisted of a stop at the wilderness outhouse, rebuilding and stoking the fire and eating. Gabrielle was captivated by the raft of birds that had gathered at the bear carcass the past few days. Ravens, magpies and camp robbers chattered, squawked and fought over the freezing carcass. On occasion a bald eagle participated. The birds kept Gabrielle entertained as she enjoyed watching, listening to and photographing them. Her collection of photos grew daily. She thought she'd have quite a menagerie from which to do a thorough article…perhaps more than one.

Lane told her, "Birds aren't the only ones eating on the bear. Predators show up at night. Their tracks indicate coyote, marten and a wolverine." Though he didn't tell Gabrielle, he thought about placing a couple of snares along game trails leading to the carcass.

Picking up his rifle, some parachute cord, snowshoes and the water bucket, Lane told Gabrielle he was going to check the snares.

He suggested she not be alarmed if she heard a rifle report.

Lane checked the first two snares to find no activity. On his way to the third snare, he noted movement in the woods and threw his rifle up to his shoulder to look through the scope. It was a moose browsing just beyond the bank of the frozen river about eighty yards away. "At last," he thought, "meat that will provide all the nourishment we need." He walked to a tree and took a rest against its trunk. He aimed just behind the moose's eye and lightly nudged the trigger back.

At the crack of the .338 the moose dropped like a sledged steer. Lane put on his snowshoes to walk over the snow to the downed animal.

Halfway to the moose he came to a slight swale in the landscape. He drew closer. To his amazement he discovered a trail. Snowshoe tracks. *Holy smokes!* He was almost beside himself with excitement. He studied the tracks and realized they represented more than a singular event—they signified a regularly used trail. He assumed that the trail was most likely that of a trapper, and understood immediately the significance of his find. He thought "Won't Gabrielle be surprised!"

He walked over to the moose and noted the hole in its head and vapor rising from the warm carcass. It was dead so he hurried back to camp. He knew the importance of butchering the moose before it froze, and he needed Gabrielle's help. But more importantly he was excited to tell her about the trap line trail.

While placing wood on the fire, Gabrielle heard the rifle's report. It startled her a bit and she wondered what kind of news Lane would have for her. She hoped he was okay. She left the campfire's comfort and walked up the river a short distance from camp. Within minutes she saw Lane moving toward her.

He hailed with a hearty, "Hey, Angel Eyes, I've got a job for you." She had some difficulty making out his exact words from the distance but briefly fantasized, hoping he was saying, "Hey, Angel Eyes, I've got the hots for you."

As Lane drew closer, he repeated himself and she realized she had misunderstood. She shrugged off her disappointment and momentarily wondered if she was going to regret the rifle shot.

He reached her and said, "I hope you won't mind, but I've just stocked our freezer for the winter. Can you help me take care of a moose?"

Ambivalent with joy for a source of food yet saddened by the death of the animal, Gabrielle answered, "You know I will, Lane. It's been a while since I've worked on an animal, but I'm at your disposal."

"Okay," Lane's voice directed, "we'll need the axe, a little cord and your snowshoes. We'll cut off quarters leaving the hide on and drag them back one at a time. I can skin each one at camp to save time and take advantage of the heat from the fire. Maybe you can carry the bucket for the heart and liver."

He told her he had a surprise for her. She asked him if it was about the moose, and he said, "No, it's something I found on the way to the moose."

Totally baffled and unable to guess what his secret was, she grabbed the bucket. Having gathered the essentials, Lane helped her put on her snowshoes and they shoed toward the moose. Gabrielle kept pestering Lane about his secret, but he merely smiled and said, "I can't say unless you guess."

When they reached the trap line, Lane asked Gabrielle to guess what it was. She said it was obvious it was a trail of some sort and asked, "But what does it mean?"

He explained, "It's a trap line trail. A trapper has to be on this stretch of river. All we have to do now is wait for him to show up. Then we can go to his cabin with him. Then we're home free. How about that!"

He explained to her that it hadn't been snowshoed for several days judging from the amount of snow on the trail, "I saw snowshoe tracks under a spruce tree over there. Most trappers run their lines in 3-day to one week cycles. He should be by any day. As soon as we take care of the moose, we'll rig up a sign. Then he'll know we're in the neighborhood."

Gabrielle was excited, "Oh, Lane, do you realize what this means? We'll be out of here in no time. Our parents won't be so worried about us." Strangely, however, inside she was dreading the end of her time with Lane. She was thinking "What if I never see him again?" Things have gone wonderfully with Lane. He's a perfect gentleman. And I sure want to get to know him better. Even if it means breaking my engagement to Marcus. Maybe...maybe the two of us...

Lane interrupted her thoughts, "Let's get to the moose and take care of it. Then we can dream about our rescue."

They reached the moose and Lane removed his snowshoes. Using the toes of one as a shovel, he dug out the snow immediately around the moose to facilitate his and Gabrielle's movement.

With Gabrielle's help Lane cut around the front and rear legs on one side. They removed them one at a time, severing the hind quarter at the hip ball joint. He placed each quarter on the snow.

Next Lane instructed Gabrielle, "Grab the front leg by the ankle, and I'll grab the hind leg so we can pull the moose onto its other side." They repeated the quarter removal process and placed the two quarters on the snow next to the first ones. As they pushed the big ungulate onto its chest, Lane explained, "I want to skin the spinal area from the neck back to get at the back strap. We'll cut that out then get the heart and liver."

Having removed the back strap, Lane took the axe and hacked at the rib cage just beneath where the foreleg would have been. He cut through three ribs at the top and bottom then took his knife to get at the heart and liver. Knowing there wasn't enough room for both the liver and the heart, he placed the heart into the bucket. *I'll save the tenderloins for last.*

He said, "I'll drag the quarters to the plane. Maybe you can carry the heart. When I come back for the next quarter, maybe you can bring the bucket for the liver."

Gabrielle responded, "Sounds good to me."

They put on their snowshoes and started for the plane, Lane pulling a hind quarter and Gabrielle carrying the bucket.

On their return to the moose they stopped at the spring where Lane rinsed as much blood from the bucket as he could. At the moose he left the pail for their last trip. Lane pulled a hind quarter as Gabrielle dragged one of the front shoulders. On the third and final trip Lane set the liver in the bucket, which lapped over the side. Lane knew it would be awkward to carry. Gabrielle picked up the bucket as Lane grabbed the last quarter. They shuffled off toward the plane, stopping every hundred feet so Gabrielle could switch hands.

When they reached camp, Lane said, "This is pretty primitive, but we'll just have to manage as well as we can. We'll skin the moose before the hide freezes solid to the meat. Then we'll store the meat under the snow and hope the critters won't bother it. We can get it out and either thaw what we need or chop off a chunk with the axe. Looks like we'll have our choice of two entrees—either fried or roast moose...or roast or fried moose. Actually we could smoke some jerky. It won't be too tasty without salt, but it's food. And, of course, we can return for the ribs and have roast ribs. Might be a good time for you to practice your New York culinary skills...if you can make this moose meat tasty without seasoning, you may be able to trade your camera in for a chef's toque.

"I'll take care of this meat and store it today then I'll follow the trap line down river tomorrow to see what I can find." He labored with the four quarters, skinning around each, setting the meat on the snow and placing the hides separately on the snow with the hair side down.

Then Lane sliced the steaks from the entire backstrap and placed a few on the roasting rack. He told Gabrielle, "The heat and smoke will combine to cook the meat. We'll play it by ear each day as to how much to cook."

Utilizing the survival gear Lane made a sign with the word "HELP" on it in large letters and an arrow designating their location.

Then he went to the snowshoe trail by the moose carcass. He tied a piece of parachute cord to each top of the note then wrapped each piece of cord to a tree on either side of the trail. He made sure it was high enough for a moose to pass under without disturbing it.

He returned to camp determined to cut and haul more wood than Gabrielle would need until his return the next afternoon. After completing that they sat around the fire until dark then crawled into the Beaver for the night.

Bright and early the next morning Lane explained to Gabrielle his plans for following the trap line trail downstream in search of the trapper's base cabin. He figured he had roughly eight hour's daylight so, "I'll travel four hours one way before turning back. You have food, water, heat, the rifle and the Beaver if you need protection from the elements or, God forbid, any disoriented Sasquatch. Will you be okay?"

Gabrielle said, "I'll be okay. You know, I'll keep busy sawing wood, tending the fire, cooking meat or jotting in my diary. You're joking about Sasquatch, right? Do you think you'll have any problems?"

Lane reassured her, "Yes, I'm kidding about Bigfoot. I'll be okay. The main thing is to keep warm without perspiring. I'll have food. I have my fire making stuff and a clear trail to follow. I can't think of any problems." He knew snowshoe travel and maneuvering the webs was sometimes cumbersome, but he didn't tell her that. Nor did he mention his need to avoid overflow, rotten ice and to keep out of reach of cantankerous moose. Knowing wolves could appear, he warned her to keep an eye out for them, just in case.

Lane said, "Gabrielle, if you saw any wood, please leave it and I'll haul it later."

He put together two roasted rabbit legs and a couple of strips of moose, stuffed the meat in a leftover zip lock baggy and pocketed the meat in his coat. As he slipped his mittens back on, he instructed her to ignite the signal pile if a plane was near, using the kindling and torch he'd prepared. They'd already gone over the use of the Skyblazer flares. Lane climbed into his snowshoes, tucked the flare gun into his waist band and told Gabrielle good-bye.

He turned and started to leave. She grabbed his coat sleeve and said, "Just a minute, Cowboy. Since you're going to be at the office all day, don't I at least get a good-bye hug?"

Lane turned to her and reached his arms around her. He said, "Okay, Missy." Knowing all he had was a stocking cap, Lane said, "I'll put on my Stetson stocking cap. But just remember that it takes more than a cowboy hat to make you a cowboy."

She clutched him tightly, and he wondered if she wasn't a little more concerned than she let on. "Gabrielle, you've trusted me so far. Trust me now. I be the pilot; you be the damsel in distress. I'll come back to you. I promise."

He dropped his arms, removed his mittens and leaned over. He gently held her chin in his left hand. With his right hand he pushed her tresses back under her stocking cap. looked into her eyes and repeated, "I'll come back to you." Then he gently kissed her on her left cheek.

He turned and started toward the trail, setting a time and land eating pace. Lane whistled "The Happy Wanderer" while his snowshoes whisked him away. Gabrielle listened to him until she could hear him whistling no longer. He turned as he entered the woods and waved, and she watched him snowshoe out of sight.

Only then did Gabrielle consider the thoughts haunting her since his announcement the night before...*Will anything happen to me? Will he be okay? Will he, in fact, be back?* She knew she must do something to get her mind off of him and his safety. She grabbed the parachute cord and rifle and headed toward the wood pile, determined to saw wood and bring some back...if she could pull it.

10

Lane's Discovery

Lane moved silently along over the snow, eyes piercing the undergrowth for any sign of the trapper or his cabin. He'd been two hours on the trail and crossed several sets. A few had fur bearers in them. Lane wondered why the trapper hadn't returned for them since it appeared they were at least a week old.

He kept reminding himself to watch for dangers along the way. He told himself more than once that he had to take care of himself. He was not only concerned for his safety but also for Gabrielle's...*her safety is nearly 100% dependent upon me.*

He kept a steady, ever vigilant, mile eating pace. He'd seen a number of moose, assuring him of the plentitude of game in the country. He rounded a bend in the trail and noticed a break ahead. When he reached it, he spotted a path leading away from the main trail.

Ten yards off the trail was a small line cabin. He hailed, "Hello the cabin." Lane expected no response and got none. His knowledge of the North told him the cabin would have little in the way of essentials. He walked over to it and cracked the door, "Anyone home?" Again, no response.

He shoved the door open all the way and poked his head inside. Peering into the dark cavern, he noticed a crude table, a partial box of candles and a box of matches. A couple of skinning-stretcher boards leaned against the far wall in one corner beyond a low pile of straw. Above the straw a rolled sleeping bag hung from a rabbit snare. The other corner sheltered a barrel stove and a stack of split firewood.

Lane knew this 8x10-foot cabin was merely a shelter from the weather, nothing more than an overnight stop for the trapper running his line.

Knowing that he had but a little over an hour remaining before his return time, he closed the door and moved on down the river. Finding the line cabin convinced Lane that the trapper's base cabin was probably at least another eight hours away. He tried to guess how long the trap line was and how many cabins the trapper had.

Lane pushed on for another hour before turning back. He thought about Gabrielle and wondered how she'd take his absence: *She must be pretty lonely...probably pretty scared. I hated to leave her alone like that but we must try to find rescue if at all possible. I'll get back to her and see if she's up to having me go upstream tomorrow.* His return trip was uneventful, and he sliced along toward camp just as daylight was waning.

Lane gave a sharp whistle when he came in view of the Beaver. He whistled a couple of more times until he saw Gabrielle leave the cargo hold, her slender figure silhouetted against the campfire. *She's so fine...5'5", 130, hazel eyes, mid-back auburn hair, ample bosom... golleee! I'll bet that's the way mom looked at that age, except for the height.*

She looked toward him, recognized his whistle, shrieked in excitement and ran for him as fast as she could.

When Gabrielle was within ear shot, Lane jokingly called out, "Honey, I'm home."

When she was a stride away, she launched herself into the air toward him. Lane braced himself and caught her, barely able to keep from falling. With tears in her eyes but a look of determination she threw her arms around him.

Gabrielle said, "I'm never letting you go again. I was going bonkers, Lane. I was wondering if you were okay. I kept praying you'd get back. I was so worried! And I'm so glad you're back."

He let her down gently onto the snow and told her he was glad to be back too. "I'm sorry, Gabrielle. I know it must have been terribly hard on you knowing your survival was fully dependent upon me."

"I can't express my anguish. I tried to keep busy but as the day wore on, so did my concern. It will be a cold day in the Devil's living room before I let you go again."

"I'm really sorry, Gabrielle. But it's my responsibility to try everything to get us out." Telling her he was famished, he teased, "Has the woman of the house a dinner for her hard working lord and master?"

They walked to the fire where they could absorb its heat. Gabrielle got into his teasing mood and asked, "Would you like a cup of coffee, Master?"

"Yes, please. That would be great, Gabrielle."

She poured his water, added a half teaspoon of coffee and stirred. Then she handed him the cup and reached toward the roasting rack, asking him, "Would you prefer filet mignon or barbecued hasenpfeffer?"

"I'll have a moose entree and rabbit for dessert," he said.

Gabrielle placed pieces of each in his camp cookware, brought it to him and sat down beside him. She queried, "So, what did you find, O, Mighty Master?"

Lane explained that he'd seen several moose and found the line cabin about two hours downstream. He explained that, "A trapper usually has a few cabins along his trap line that he utilizes to get out of the weather or perhaps to skin his catch. Such shelters are about a day's journey from each other. Depending upon the length of the trap line a trapper could have up to a dozen line cabins; but normally he has less than six. Most trap lines are less than a hundred miles long." He told her it was probable that there was another cabin upstream eight to ten hours away. Aware of her distress by his absence, however, he said nothing about going in that direction.

As the cloak of darkness enveloped them, they sat and enjoyed the warmth and firelight in each other's company.

Gabrielle felt comfort with Lane's safe return. A plethora of thoughts affronted her while thinking of the past few days...What's happening to me? Am I hallucinating? I find myself questioning my beliefs. We've discussed killing and eating animals. I've helped gut and quarter a moose, I've eaten part of it. I'm confused.

Lane interrupted her thoughts, "It's warming up. It feels like snow. I guess we can hit the sack and see what tomorrow brings. Is there anything I can do for you before we go to bed?"

While Gabrielle thought about Lane's kind and gentle nature, she fantasized about his question...What would I like him to do for me? Then she shook her head and said, "No, I guess not. Not yet, anyway."

Lane volunteered, "How about if I massage your back and shoulders? Kelly taught me how to do that. We periodically exchange back massages."

Gabrielle was all too eager to accept but she acted coy, "That would be nice, Lane."

She removed her coat, unzipped her coveralls and pulled her sweater over her head, exposing her blouse. She turned her back to Lane.

Lane placed a hand on each shoulder and began gently kneading each one. His hands moved toward her neck. Then he placed one thumb above the other on her spine at the base of her skull and pushed against the vertebra, moving his fingers rhythmically in circular motions on either side of her neck.

He worked down her neck to her trapezius muscles and across to her shoulders before he returned to her spine. Then he placed a hand on either trap muscle and worked her spinal column below her neck with his thumbs, pushing tenderly.

Gabrielle involuntarily emitted soft "oohhh's" as he worked down her back, kneading either side in ever enlarging circular motions. Thoroughly enjoying the massage, she relaxed.

After ten minutes Lane stopped and said, "Okay, Angel Eyes, that's going to have to do for now. I'm bushed and need all the beauty rest I can get. What do you say? Is there anything else before we're bedroom bound?"

"I'd race you to the plane," she said, "but I'm too relaxed. Maybe you could carry me there and put me into bed."

"Now, you're taking advantage of this country boy. Don't try turning me into your butler." Lane dragged a log to the fire and placed it over the burning chunks of driftwood and glowing coals. He followed Gabrielle to the plane, noticing his shadow masking the dancing reflections cast on the skin of the Beaver by the orange firelight.

He climbed into the plane and said, "Okay, now. Don't be a bed hog tonight. I deserve just as much room as you do. Besides, I'm more tired than you."

Gabrielle whispered, "Don't bother me. I'm asleep, waiting for a handsome prince to kiss me so I can live happily ever after."

In jest Lane said, "Dream on." Then he added, "Good night, sweet Princess."

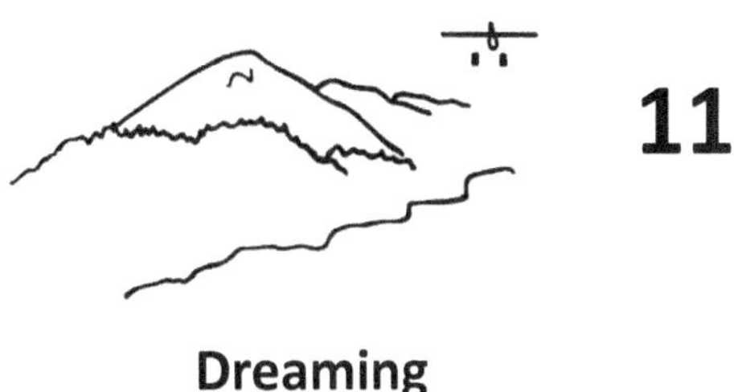

11

Dreaming

Gabrielle and Lane awakened the next morning with anticipation of a good day. They were surprised to discover three inches of new snow on the ground. The amount would not hinder their activities, but it would prevent pilots from seeing the plane.

They filed out of the plane to begin their day. As usual they were bundled in their layers of clothing—underwear, pants, shirt, sweater, coveralls, coat, mittens or gloves and stocking caps.

While Gabrielle went to the outhouse, Lane busied himself. He breathed new life into the fire. Blowing gently on the remaining coals, he placed kindling on them. Blue smoke rose stubbornly above the smoldering wood. Within moments flames leaped from one piece of kindling to the next as a roaring fire lurched to life.

Happy with the fire's success, he cut a spruce limb from a nearby tree and raked the snow off the tarp. He knew it would be more difficult removing the snow from the plane, but he walked around swishing snow from the wings and the fuselage.

Before long Gabrielle was back. While she stood by the fire's warmth rubbing her hands together and doing jumping jacks, Lane excused himself and left for the privacy of the outhouse.

Returning, Lane washed his hands with snow and warmed them by the fire. Then he asked her, "Like a cup of tea with breakfast?"

"Yes, thanks."

He passed her the tea. So far they'd been able to use the tea bags at full strength, but saved each for a second or third using just in case rescue took longer. Then he handed her a camp kit bowl with warm moose meat.

Becoming more comfortable with the idea of eating meat Gabrielle responded, "Thank you, Lane."

As they'd done each day so far, they planned their activities for the next dozen hours. These always included several attempts to raise someone on the plane's radio. Lane said, "I think we should look along the bank for Labrador tea plants; we can make tea from that. The snow's so deep it will be hard to find. But we might find some under the shelter of the trees. We'll cut some spruce branches for spruce needle tea."

Knowing about the military's efforts to keep up morale by maintaining a clean barracks, Lane did his best to keep a clean camp. Beyond that, he encouraged Gabrielle, reassuring her that they would survive. He invented a whole series of games aimed at keeping her mind off their dilemma. Some of the games were mental, some were physical, like relays or building objects such as the roasting rack and a drying rack near the fire, a place where they could put wet clothes.

He continually encouraged her to think of accessories that he could make for their living room-kitchen. He also asked her to let him know if there was something she wanted him to do. And they both kept an eye on the plane and the tarp. Keeping the snow off the plane and the tarp anchored was routine, varying only when the weather brought wind or snow.

While finishing breakfast Gabrielle asked, "Lane, why did you become a pilot?"

"It's kind of a long story. Want the short or the long version?"

Gabrielle answered, "You know, since we're not going anywhere, the long version works fine for me."

Lane began, "I grew up with the outdoors. My father always took the family on outings. Some of my best memories are of our family's camping, clamming, fishing, hiking and hunting trips. If you get real bored later, ask me to tell you about some of our family trips, like fishing the Russian River, dip netting in the Copper River, clamming Cook Inlet or straggling along behind my dad on Dall sheep hunts... now there's a workout.

"Because of dad's flying and family friends who have airplanes, I developed a desire to fly. I took aviation science in high school and got my license. From there I worked toward my instrument and multi-engine ratings.

"Back in the late '70's dad learned about some surplus military Beavers in crates. No one was interested in them then—it was before they got popular with air taxi operators. Dad's enterprising zeal led him to buy two of them for something like twelve grand each. He commercial fished summers to pay for them.

"He hung onto one as an investment and converted the other from military application for his own use. He made a lot of modifications such as moving and coordinating the fuel selector with the fuel gauge, adding steel springs on the wheel-skis and installing newer instrumentation.

A couple of dad's former students networked with Beaver experts they knew. That's how dad got his conversion. Incidentally, he came up with the tail numbers one-niner-six-niner Bravo because I was born in '69; and he says my sisters and I were raised to be brave.

"When I started flying more than dad, he let me use his *Tundra Bunny* to get my Beaver rating. I've been flying her ever since."

"When you explained your father's desire to name *Tundra Bunny* for your mother, I thought maybe it was a chauvinistic male thing but I consider it admirable that he honored her this way. I'm glad you explained it."

"Well, all I can say is that before you label all of us males, you need to get to know some of us a little better. We're not all beer guzzling, TV sports junkies."

"I'm beginning to see that."

Lane continued, "Dad's other Beaver is still in a crate in our barn, getting more valuable by the year. A Beaver in prime condition is worth around three hundred grand on today's market. Don't know how long dad will sit on it."

Gabrielle asked, "Since you're flying your dad's plane, is it like you own it?"

"Sort of. Maybe dad is planning to let me buy it from him some day."

"If it's kind of your plane," said Gabrielle, "then why did you have me check with the dispatcher to see if I could go with you?"

"Because I knew she'd say 'yes,' and I was doing the procedure thing, trying to be professional. I flew a couple of summers for AirLaska as a contract pilot. I was offered a full time job after I graduated from college. It seemed like a good way to make some money and to pay off my college bills before going back for my masters degree, so I accepted. Is that version long enough?"

"Yes. Just fine, thank you. So you've been flying a few years?"

"Since I was 14-years-old, actually. I've flown full time two summers and three years full time."

"So, when are you planning to return to college and what are your future plans?"

He teased her, "Oh, I've decided to bag college. I'll return from this outing a world famous bush pilot. Your photo-essay will be worth millions. You'll be so grateful for the recognition, that you'll share your millions with me. I'll invest it in my own air taxi. You'll be so pleased that you'll put me on $100,000 a year retainer to fly you all over Alaska for your work. You'll include my flight service in all your stories; I'll become almost as famous as you, and filthy-rich clients will pour into my office from all over the world."

She jabbed him and said, "Be serious. I am. Come on, Lane, what do you plan to do with your life?"

"Actually, I plan to teach at the college level. I want to pursue my doctorate then apply at a university where I can work with young people. It will take a few more years, but I'm getting there. This could be my last year of flying for a living. But I may fly summers between teaching years. I'll have to wait and see."

Lane grinned and turned to her. "Now it's your turn, Angel Eyes. Are you going to be a career woman forever? Will you be the female Ansel Adams?"

"I don't really know. I like to read. And I really enjoy hiking and rappelling."

"Whoa!" Lane interrupted, "Rappelling? Where'd you pick that up?"

"I'm an Outward Bound graduate in mountain skills and saltwater kayaking. That's how I knew about freeze dried food. I thoroughly enjoy the outdoors, so you see, Mister Smarty Pants, you've got more than a spoiled New Yorker on your hands."

"Wow! And I thought you were just another woman tourist. Not just another in the beauty department, however."

"Yes, when I first came to Alaska, I dreamed of being the female Ansel Adams. Dad started me on photography and I've loved it ever since. After junior high my mother sent me to a private school in Europe. I learned proper protocol, manners and civility, political views including correctness. Every summer I returned to New York until my senior year. That summer I traveled Europe, and on succeeding summers I traveled various parts of the world, my camera always beside me. I graduated college with grandiose ideas about my future. I wanted to tell the world about the awful injustices and exploitations perpetrated against animals and peoples. I told myself I was born to spread the news and open eyes.

"I'm having second thoughts, now, however. I'm not sure how long I want to pursue any career. I've learned a lot in the past few days. I need to give it more time and thought. Daily I'm learning more about what really matters in my life.

"I'm concerned about our plight. I know it must be affecting my parents a great deal. I want to get out of here. I want to thank them for all they've done for me. And I want to start living...really living."

"I know this experience has been tough on you, Gabrielle. I take full responsibility for our situation. I intend to see you back to safety, back to your parents. I won't let you down."

"I know you won't, Lane. You've done and are doing everything you can. Your efforts to keep me up emotionally have been precious to me." Thinking about how much she was falling for him and knowing that she couldn't tell him, she added as an after thought, "The way you've helped me has meant more to me than I can tell you."

Then he asked the question she knew would come, "What about

your fiancé?"

"We're engaged with a September wedding date," she replied haltingly. "But, honestly, I've thought of Marcus very little since our outing began. You know, Lane, things change. I didn't think it was possible, but it's happening to me. Many of my long-held, deeply entrenched ideas are under assault. I thought I had figured out everything, but now I'm really wondering..."

"Wondering is a good thing. We often run into blind canyons that require us to try to figure a way out. We have to play the fish that happens to be on our lines. We've got to fly our own planes—there's no auto pilot in life. You're at an exciting crossroads in your life. You have questions. You'll find answers."

Gabrielle smiled and responded, "Lane, you always seem to say the right thing, and do the right thing. I admire that."

From the beginning Gabrielle noticed that Lane did not wear a wedding band. He had told her that he lived with his parents, but she was curious to know if there was a girl in his life. Wanting to change the subject from herself and ever curious about Lane's plans, she asked, "So, what about you...do you have someone special in your future?"

"At the moment there are three women hounding me to marry them. I'm having a rough time deciding because one is beautiful but broke; one is ugly but rich; and the third is beautiful and rich. The beautiful, poor one is my 3-year-old niece. The ugly-rich one spends the night with me every once in a while...in my nightmares. And the beautiful and rich one is my 84-year-old grandmother."

"Oh, Lane. Stop teasing me. I'm serious."

"Okay, okay. I'll try to be more serious. Sometimes I think you're too serious. Can't you lighten up?" Ever since he'd first seen her, he had been thinking about Gabrielle and wondering if she fit into his life in a role different from a client. He wanted to tell her how he felt about her but he didn't think it prudent at this time—he hadn't come up with an answer yet and he didn't want to lead her on. Besides she was an engaged woman.

After a long pause he told her, "Actually there's this beautiful woman I met once. We were stranded on an Island. She was so fine. About 5'6" tall and 135 pounds with a great body. Her hazel eyes lit up a room, auburn hair rippled like golden-red wheat in the summer wind. The only thing bad about her was that she was from New York."

Gabrielle jumped on him and tried to tickle him through his thick clothes. "You big joker!" She kept tickling him as they rolled off the couch and onto the ground. She was wondering if he actually thought she was beautiful, when suddenly they came to rest with Lane pancaked on top of her.

He rolled to his knees, resting his weight on either side of her, cupping her head in his strong right hand. With his left hand he re-arranged her stocking cap, parted a few errant strands of hair from her face and looked into her eyes. An almost overwhelming desire to kiss her pink, soft lips swept over him. But he thought better of it. He kissed her on the cheek then clasped her gloved hands in his and pulled her upright.

"Now that you've severely damaged my tickle organs and who knows what else, I'll probably have to be more serious."

Gabrielle laughed as they moved back to the couch.

"What are you looking for in a woman?" she asked.

He thought long about her question, especially because he found more and more in her that he liked. In his mind he sorted over his list of criteria for a wife.

His check list was one he had been developing since before high school. "Several things matter most to me when it comes to women. The first three or four are pretty well set in concrete. After that I'm looking for a woman with as many positive qualities as possible."

"Like, what for example?" she asked.

"My perfect woman would have to share my faith in God." Lane explained that he'd like a woman like his mother. "She would want to rear a strong, close-knit family. My mother is the closest example I can point to of a saint. She has always loved her faith, passed it on to her children, does so with her granddaughter, the remainder of her family and friends. Not in an overbearing way, but in a loving manner. My wife could share my mother's ways, and I'd be extremely happy.

"Next, fidelity. I want a wife who is loyal to me, one who wouldn't think of running off with someone else. One who would realize that when the storms came, which they do in marriage just as in other aspects of life, that we'd make up our minds to weather them and not abandon ship. A woman like that would be a treasure.

"Personality is critical. A wife who can laugh but be serious would be a great asset. We have too many people who take life too seriously.

"A good mother, a good conversationalist...a good cook. All those would be frosting on the cake. And I want a woman who came from a stable home.

"Marriage is wonderful when you're with the right partner. The romance of dating often fizzles after marriage. Many of my friends no longer buy gifts for their wives, even simple things like flowers and candy. They have trouble saying 'I love you.' Their pre-marriage hidden habits creep in...things like belching.

"I guess my greatest concern is that I won't measure up as a husband, the fear of failure. I'll never make a commitment to a woman then let her down."

There was a pause before he spoke again, "Your turn again,

Gabrielle. What do you want in a good husband?"

She replied, "Not just a handsome hunk. I'd prefer a stable man, a man who's secure in himself, whom I could depend on, even in a life and death situation. I, too, want a spouse who is faithful. I want a kind, considerate, thoughtful, understanding man, one who knows how to treat a woman. Gentle. Strong, yet able to cry and admit his mistakes."

She knew these qualities fit Lane. "I want a man with confidence, one who knows who he is and isn't concerned about his baldness or the color of his hair...a man who is competent, one who can get things done, and who takes control...without being a dictator.

"My husband will be a guy who loves kids and treats his children and his wife with equal respect. I won't settle for anything less."

"Does Marcus fill the bill?"

"As for Marcus, I'm having more and more doubts and second thoughts..."

"Wow!" Lane stated with conviction, "You know what you want. If Marcus is out of the picture, do you think you'll ever find your dream guy?"

"I think I already have," she risked. "I'm working on it. I'll let you know as soon as I know for sure."

"I guess we'd better try to find that tea and cut some spruce branches for our dietary supplement," Lane said. "Do you want to help me or stay here?"

"I'll go with. Think it will take long?"

"If we don't find the Labrador tea, we can always get spruce needles which are abundant all around us. Shouldn't take more than an hour."

They put on their snowshoes, Lane grabbed the saw and the flare gun and they left camp headed toward the spring.

While moving toward a pocket of spruce, Lane brushed against some low snow covered bushes knocking the snow from them. He was excited to discover Labrador tea bushes. He cut several entire bushes and handed them to Gabrielle saying, "You'll be surprised how good this tea is."

"How do you fix it?"

"Basically you just add the leaves to the hot water, and the wonderful flavor seeps in. You'll see."

Beneath her mantle of tea branches Gabrielle looked like a miniature oak tree. They snowshoed to a spruce tree where she waited for Lane to saw through a low limb. Lane shouldered the limb and turned toward Gabrielle. Suddenly he noticed bushes grouped tightly near a huge cottonwood tree. He hurriedly dropped the spruce limb and saw, shouting excitedly, "Hey, we've got rose hips! Want to come see these beauties, Gabrielle?"

A couple of downed spruce trees leaned against the cottonwood, sheltering the ground somewhat from the preceding snowfalls. Snow was only half as deep as the surrounding area. Lane said, "Looks like we're being taken care of on all fronts."

He snowshoed a short distance and discovered a veritable trove of rose bushes. He began picking the frozen, thumb-sized rose hips from waist-high bushes. Realizing they could probably get rose hips for quite a while, he told Gabrielle, "There's probably some buried under the snow which we can use as our freezer. You'll love these. They're full of Vitamin C."

They gathered a few handfuls of the hips and put them in their pockets, and Gabrielle commented, "They look kind of like shriveled, miniature red pears."

Returning to the spruce limb and the saw, Lane picked them up. He turned to Gabrielle and together they retraced their steps to camp.

He fetched a beaver blanket from the plane and returned to sit alongside Gabrielle. He showed her how to remove the tea leaves then stoked the fire with another log. Together they stripped the leaves from the bush and placed them on the blanket for future use. When they finished that, they started stripping the spruce branch of its needles and placing them in a zip lock bag.

Lane told her that the rose hips could be eaten plain or added to water for a drink. He also told her that the rose leaves made a pleasant, mild tea.

Gabrielle said, "Our pantry is brimming with goodies."

Even though she was somewhat sarcastic, Lane was pleased to observe her obvious joy. They had come a long way the past few days in securing a food supply and establishing a permanent shelter in circumstances that could be much worse.

Lane added, "Yes, if this river weren't frozen, we could probably supplement our rations with fish."

"You mentioned family trips earlier, including fishing. What was that like?" she asked.

"Well, we used to fish the Russian River before it became a park and was inundated with people. We dip netted the Copper and Kenai rivers. Last summer dad, Kelly, my brother-in-law Brad and I drove to the mouth of the Kenai with our friend Hieu Le and a couple of his nephews visiting from California.

"We bounced over the sand a mile or so to the river and we fished the high tide even though it was a couple of hours before dawn. We pulled on our chest waders and head lamps and headed out into the surf in the pitch black, dancing against the incoming breakers. It was ghostly eerie not knowing what the darkness held. The wind lashed the pounding waves around us. One wave almost washed Frank, Hieu's older nephew, out before we had a chance to warn him of the danger. A wall of water bellowed up in front of me, and I turned my back to it as it cascaded over my head. I was glad I was wearing a rain coat over my waders. At that point we decided to scrunch back up the incline closer to the beach.

"Basically we all just hefted our nets out into the current, dropping the net end into the surf. At first we pulled the nets downstream because the tide held them steady. But later all we had to do was drop the net and let the river current push the net downstream. The better nets have twelve to fifteen foot handles; however some people add an extension or make their own with a wider mouth and add gill net webbing which the fish can't see.

"We caught a couple dozen red salmon, called sockeye by the cannery people. We cleaned them and put them in our coolers before returning to town. Then we repeated tradition and stopped at Sourdough Sal's Klondike City for breakfast in Soldotna.

"It's always fun watching newcomers like Frank catch salmon. And always rewarding watching visitors enjoy the Great Land. It reminds me of a trip dad made to the Russian before I was born and before there was even a road into the campground. Dad, his friend Chester Meeks, dad's brother-in-law Les Smothers and his father Lester senior went to a hot spot. Dad wanted the visitors to catch fish so badly that on the way to the river he prayed that Les and his dad would limit out, even if dad didn't catch a fish. Guess what?"

Gabrielle responded, "They all caught their limits."

"No," Lane replied, "everyone caught his limit except dad. He never caught a fish. To add humiliation to his embarrassment, he managed to kick the biggest salmon off Grandpa Smothers' line in his effort to beach it."

Gabrielle launched a new subject, "I've noticed you reading a book off and on. What's it about?"

"I'll go get it." Lane went to retrieve his Hebrew Old Testament from the cockpit. When he returned, he said, "It's a book about the history of baseball. Want me to read you some information from it?"

"Sure, why not."

Lane read Genesis 1:1 in Hebrew. Obviously Gabrielle didn't know what it said, and Lane asked, "Do you want me to interpret?"

"Yes."

Lane said, "It says, 'In the big inning.' I told you it was about baseball."

"You're kidding me again."

"Yes," he said, "I am. It says, 'In the beginning.' This book is one that I keep studying so I won't forget my Hebrew. It's a Hebrew Old Testament. I need to have a grasp of Hebrew in order to pursue my schooling; and I don't want to get stale."

Gabrielle said, "You said earlier that you wanted to teach at the college level. Do you know where?"

"I'm not sure where. I will teach philosophy and Biblical studies, offered at only a handful of universities Outside. I want to share with others the search for truth. I want to explain the concepts of truth as presented in the Bible."

Gabrielle asked, "Would you give up your love of Alaska and all the adventure and experiences to teach? Why wouldn't you want to stay here and teach something else?"

"I can't answer your question with a simple response. I need to give you some background. I know women want men to be good listeners, but I hope you'll forgive my long-winded explanation.

"Life is full of sacrifices. Think about the woman who endures pain before and during childbirth for the sake of having children. She sacrifices her body. And what about the people who give their lives for others? Do you know the story of the praying hands?"

"No, tell me."

"As I understand it, around 1500 two brothers wanted to become artists. They were the sons of Albrecht Durer the Elder who had eighteen children. Since they could not afford for both to attend the Academy in Nuremberg, they agreed one would work in the mines to financially support the winner of a tossed coin. Albert went to the mines; Albrecht went to the Academy. When accomplished artist Albrecht returned home and announced it was Albert's turn to go to the academy, Albert kindly declined. He didn't think his injured and arthritic hands would master the training. In a gesture of love and gratitude, Albrecht drew his brother's hands in a praying position to honor Albrecht's loving sacrifice. Even if it's fiction, it's a story of true sacrifice and love, don't you think?"

"Yes, it is. It would be rare for that to happen in our society today."

"You're right. But don't you think if more people practiced the teachings of Jesus, we'd see more kindness?"

"I don't know if I've ever thought much about it."

Lane continued, "Jesus practiced what he preached. He was God in human flesh. Do you think He wanted to go to Golgotha and be hanged from a cross for the sins of the world? Because He loved mankind, He sacrificed His desires and His life for all of us."

Gabrielle interjected, "Growing up I attended Sunday school and church nearly every Sunday. But all that changed with my brother's death. It seemed like life was a drag for a long time. Then we never seemed to get back to church.

"When Gabe died, I turned my back on God and guns. It was emotionally traumatic accepting my father—I believed he had nothing to do with the accident, but I was bitter that God had taken my brother. And I was angry because my father couldn't prevent Gabe's death. My mother and I both turned our backs on God, but my father didn't. What you're saying is similar to what my father has told me in the past. He always said that too many people made Christianity too complex, that it was so simple that most people couldn't accept its simplicity. It makes sense."

Lane continued, "Contrary to what many people think, Jesus is not about rules and regulations. The exact opposite is true. He came to fulfill our lives, to give us direction like an older brother. Jesus gave us principles that would enable us to become our best. I don't think God wants to rule our lives, but he has rules to enrich our lives.

"Man chooses to accept or reject him. Historically, Jesus lived. Man is free to choose whether or not to believe that Jesus was everything He said He was. If a person believes that Jesus was the Savior, all he has to do is ask God to forgive him. After that the person practices the teachings of Jesus.

"It's really simple. What Christianity amounts to is a relationship between the believer and the Savior wherein the believer depends upon Jesus for daily direction and support. You don't need another person to represent you."

Gabrielle carefully considered his words and said, "I guess I still have many questions at this time. I need to keep seeking."

Lane explained, "There are many times in life when we do not know the answers. We will probably never know the answer to all our 'why's' in spite of our desire to understand. In time you will find the comfort you need."

Gabrielle thought about Lane's words and realized how much you can learn about a person while sitting with him for hours around a campfire...there's nothing to hide.

Then Gabrielle changed the subject somewhat, "Lane, if we were the only two humans on earth and we knew that tomorrow we'd die, what would you think?"

"Do you mean what do I think or what would I want to do? What I'd like to do isn't what would be best. I'd do just what we've been doing. That may not sound romantic, Gabrielle, but that's what I'd do.

"Being the last humans on earth, we could do about anything we chose to do, including snuggling skin to skin. I'd be the first man to tell you that I'm game. In a heartbeat. Selfishly it would be easy. But doing the right thing is often very difficult.

"You are extremely desirable, however I couldn't possibly take advantage of you. Even if we both wanted it. It would be an injustice to you, to me, to our families and, more importantly, to our Creator.

"Our lives are fraught with choices between good and evil, right and wrong. We have the opportunity to choose. It may sound hokey to you, but we are accountable for our actions. In order to remain pure we must be responsible to guard those actions.

"I constantly battle the desire to indulge my appetites. If I give in to my desires, I fail both of us. I choose to honor my Christian beliefs. By honoring those, goodness will prevail...and I can look you in the eyes knowing I have done you no harm, physically, emotionally or spiritually. And I can look at my reflection in the mirror and know that I have been true to my Lord, and thus to myself.

"Please," Lane concluded, "don't ever misinterpret my physical passiveness toward you as lack of interest in you."

Gabrielle blushed as Lane reached his left arm around her shoulders and drew her against his chest. Accepting his discourse she leaned her head against his shoulder.

Later that afternoon Gabrielle asked, "Lane how much longer do you think we'll have to wait for rescue?"

"Maybe the trapper will show up, perhaps even tomorrow. Most of these people have some sort of routine where they keep in touch with civilization on a regular basis. Granted that regular basis might be only twice a year, but I'm assuming this trapper probably has a bush pilot who drops stuff to him periodically. Don't worry, Gabrielle, we're going to make it."

Then as a means of encouraging her he shared a story with her, "One of my favorite survival stories, and one of the most famous to come out of the north country took place in 1963. Helen Klaben summarized their experience in the book *Hey, I'm Alive!* A pilot filed a flight plan for a trip from Fairbanks to San Francisco. He took a female passenger. Their plane crashed in the Yukon.

"Both survived but they didn't know where they were. Their supplies consisted of a few tins of sardines, tuna and fruit cocktail, some crackers, a couple of pieces of chicken, vitamins, some chocolate and toothpaste.

"They endured for forty-nine days, sometimes in weather 40 degrees below zero, before rescue came.

"They made it. Compared to them we're in Shangri-la. We'll make it. And guess what? The gal in that crash was a New Yorker!"

Within a few days of Lane's unsuccessful attempt to locate the trapper's cabin a routine of camp life began taking shape. Days turned into weeks. Lane and Gabrielle arose, used the outhouse, groomed themselves for the day, stoked the fire, cut and hauled wood, replenished their water supply, cooked and ate, tried the radio, curried camp, played games, reminisced, told stories and then went to bed.

After the first few days they saw or heard only three planes. Two flew past them before they could respond. One flew over while they were enveloped in thick ground fog. Lane wondered why there were so few planes flying.

Periodically he worked on the plane engine with his limited tools, but he could find no reason for its failure to start. Some days they checked the trap line sign.

Since they gained considerably on their wood cache, they had time on their hands. Baths became a regular activity, necessitating numerous trips to the spring. They heated the water, covered the tub to keep heat in and went for more water.

Lane fashioned "toilet paper" from dead branches and told Gabrielle it wasn't out of the question in desperation to use snow, which worked both to wipe and to clean.

While Gabrielle bathed, Lane cut wood or checked their rabbit snares. When Lane bathed, Gabrielle wrote religiously in her diary, usually in some comfort at the fur couch.

Lane and Gabrielle developed a break time, an escape from cutting and hauling wood, scrounging for edible vegetation and keeping up the camp. During this time Lane read from his Hebrew Old Testament and sometimes Gabrielle asked Lane to read aloud to her. He enjoyed that and enlightening her about his faith. She liked hearing him read because what he read gave her strength. She found comfort and solace in his voice. More and more, she was falling in love with her Alaskan Viking.

A couple of weeks after their forced landing Lane jubilantly stated, "Looks like today's wash day. Okay, Princess, empty your clothes hamper, your loyal servant is going to do the laundry."

Gabrielle was ecstatic until she thought about her under things, "I think that's a wonderful idea, laundry man. However I'll be the laundry lady and do my own underwear."

Lane dragged the tub from the plane and cleaned it as well as he could. Then they dumped their clothes into it while adding a bucket of hot water. Lane added a few more buckets of water as it heated, and he and Gabrielle "washed" their clothes, stirring them with a stick Lane had designed for the purpose. Then they hung their clothes up to dry on their drying rack near the campfire, the excess clothes going onto a temporary "clothes line" Lane had put together. His challenge was that of getting the clothes line near enough to the fire to dry the clothes before they froze, a problem he solved by shifting the clothes from the outside ends toward the middle as the interior garments dried, then repeating the process until all were dry.

While sitting on the couch Gabrielle complimented Lane on his appearance, "I think your beard's quite becoming. Do you think you'll want to keep it when we get back to civilization?'

"I'm not sure." Then, teasingly, he added, "Do you think it will help me get the woman of my dreams?"

She smiled, "I think it makes you look more rugged, more handsome." Then she blushed, "But I don't know how you could look any better—you're as handsome as can be right now."

"Gabrielle, you're embarrassing me," he said. Changing the subject and deciding to get some activity and Gabrielle's mind off their situation, he suggested,

"Let's play some hockey. We can use some sticks to form a couple of nets and others for hockey sticks. We'll slide on the river ice and use a rock for a puck. It'll be Alaska vs. New York."

"You're on, Cowboy. Maybe you think you're hot stuff, but that's probably because you never heard of the New York Rangers. You better watch yourself."

So they grabbed a rock and a couple of sticks. They laid out sticks to form "nets" on the ice about a hundred and fifty feet apart. Lane dropped the rock at the center of the "rink" and Gabrielle slapped at it. Nicking it and pushing it off center ice she charged toward it laughing with Lane in her wake. He caught her with some effort and they began running and sliding over the ice toward her goal. For an hour they "skated" back and forth whacking the rock toward each other's goal or tackling each other as one tried to shoot the "puck." Lane was amazed and challenged by Gabrielle's athleticism. Before long they left the ice for the fireside and the couch.

Lane told Gabrielle, "You're quite the athlete. Is that natural or learned?"

"I engaged in a number of sports while growing up. My father was a sports nut to a degree and involved us in back yard activities like softball, volleyball and badminton. Plus we played racquetball and occasionally basketball at his club.

"I played sports in high school and college, either varsity or intramural."

"Well, it definitely shows. You cleaned my clock out there on the ice. I kept wanting to holler to the coach for substitution, but you never gave me the chance."

Gabrielle got discouraged periodically, but Lane tried to monitor her moods to encourage her. He always cheered her up by getting her to think of something else, often by playing games or reminding her that spring was on the way and that the time would come when they could go down river if rescue failed to materialize.

Nearly a month passed with no sign of rescue. Other than that the best news was that the temperature never became unbearable. There were a few days in the minus thirty degree range and a couple that were colder with the wind chill factor, but all in all they endured the cold admirably. The tarp shielded them from the wind for the most part, and the wood supply never ran out. Lane made sure that they always had a stock pile near the fire so that they wouldn't have to deal with the cold any more than necessary. In early April the couple enjoyed warmer weather.

Lane believed it was just a matter of time before they could start building a raft that would float them to civilization. In the warmth of the spring days, he spent more time formulating a plan for constructing the raft. He knew there were dangers such as sweepers, but he chose to keep them secret until such time as Gabrielle needed to know. He thought "No reason to unduly alarm Gabrielle."

And he hoped they'd find the trapper's cabin on their downstream journey.

One of Gabrielle's diary entries read:

Dear Diary,

We've enjoyed the northern lights on a few occasions. A normal aurora is displayed in greens, from dull to bright. A green wave flows across the sky. Sometimes a violet ribbon bursts forth to accompany it.

The aurora borealis constantly changes in color and shape. One night pinks, reds and oranges shimmer the night sky. Splotches of color, wave upon wave, span the sky. The color banners move simultaneously up and down like bright roller coasters, swirling back and forth accordion-like.

Pastel lights crackle and hiss. Hundreds of serpent-tongued fingers flick out across the blue-black canopy overhead.

P.S. Who would have ever thought when I began this trek that I'd meet a stranger who would come to mean so much to me? Lane, I've discovered, is a perfect stranger.

He's so good to me, so concerned about me. Surely his attention can't be an act. If he's so genuine, why aren't more men like he?

12

The Trapper

One day about noon Lane was in the outhouse and Gabrielle was sitting on the couch writing in her diary. She looked across the river. Suddenly she stopped. Thinking she must be seeing things, she looked again, carefully. She blinked. Then she rubbed her eyes. She wondered, *Can that be a person?* She looked more closely. It was a person.

She hurriedly ran toward the outhouse, stopped nearby and, trying not to alert the stranger, hissed in a semi-urgent voice, "Lane! Lane, someone's coming!"

Hardly had she turned toward the approaching person when Lane burst from the outhouse, ran over to her and stared toward the river ice. He said, "It's probably the trapper. Looks like he's carrying a rifle."

Lane called out over the ice, "Hellooo!"

A voice floated back across mixing with Lane's echo. It sounded like, "I'm here to help!"

The man's easy, rhythmic gait belied his agelessness as he snowshoed closer. A thick down parka and wool pants covered the slight figure and a dark, brown, beaver cap crowned his head. White whiskers framed his seasoned, tanned face. His squinty eyes scoured the landscape.

As the stranger reached them, Lane ran up to him and thrust out his right hand, "Boy, are we glad to see you. Can we offer you some tea?"

Shocked to see a couple of people in this people-less vastness, the stranger looked at them in stunned awe. His smoky, blue eyes were looking at two people who had been outside the confines of civilization, staring death in the face, struggling for survival and battling semi-starvation. Forgetting the niceties of civilization, he blurted, "How long you folks been here?"

"Going on a month," Lane answered.

"Exactly twenty-nine days," Gabrielle interjected.

The trapper responded, "Geewinikers. You're kiddin' aren't you? You don't look like you could possibly have been here that long."

Gabrielle spoke up, "Trust me, twenty-nine days exactly."

"Mother Dugan!" the trapper spat. "You don't say? Now, ain't that sumthin'!" Then regaining his composure some he asked, "Anybody hurt?"

Lane replied, "Only in the pocket book. Gabrielle may be worse off financially because she has a good paying job in New York, and I'm keeping her from her work. However this experience may fit into her work since she's a writer-photographer. She'll probably write something about a crazy bush pilot giving her the scare of her life in Alaska. She might even sue me and give up her career. By the way, my name's Lane Morgan. This is Gabrielle Lacey."

The trapper pushed back his beaver hat exposing a white crest, scratched his head and said, "Pleased t' meet ya. My handle's Sam Mc Callister. My place is twenty miles down river."

They moved toward the fire where Lane poured some hot water into the fire-charred stew can. Neither Gabrielle nor Lane could help noticing Sam's face. Grooved with lines, it resembled the crinkles of a jigsaw puzzle.

Sam began jabbering away and Lane thought, *Just like all those other bush people who get cabin fever and don't have anyone to talk to all winter.*

Sam said, "I saw your sign. Geewinikers, was I surprised! Figgered I'd better get over here t' see what in tarnation it was all about."

Lane told Sam they'd found his trail and expected him sooner, "We tried to figure out why you weren't on your trap line. I walked downstream one day, but only found your line cabin."

"I've been bad sick. Don't know what it was but I couldn't get out of bed fer three days. Took me over two weeks t' get strong enough t' leave my cabin. Then I thought it was safe t' come out and pull my traps. My sled is back at the trail."

They talked about the engine failure, the landing, Lane's injury and how they'd stayed alive—including the wood and food sources, the homemade snowshoes and Gabrielle's bear.

Sam said, "I've crossed that bear's trail a few times and stayed on the look out fer it. Never wanted t' run into a cantankerous grizzly, least of all a freak one out of hibernation in winter."

After they finished their tea, Sam told them he wanted to reach his line cabin before dark and asked them what they'd like to do. He said, "I can call Anchorage on the radio and have them send out a plane fer ya. Or you're welcome t' come t' my place till a plane or chopper can get to ya."

"I'd like to go," said Gabrielle.

Lane agreed and said, "We'll go to your place. We'll take the rest of the afternoon and get our stuff together then break camp first thing in the morning. Think we'd have any problems making it to your home cabin in a day?"

"The river's pretty clear of snow," Sam responded. "You can cover most of the trail without snowshoes. Some bends have drifted snow where you'll need snowshoes. The only thing t' slow you down is yerselves. You could make it, even if it turns into a long day. You know winter nights never get real dark with the snow cover."

"That's true, Sam," said Lane. "We'll plan on being at your place tomorrow night."

Lane retrieved his aeronautical map from the plane, and Sam pointed out his cabin's location, "Geewinikers, can't miss it. Just follow the river downstream. You'll pass three large streams comin' in on the left side, and..." he pointed to the map, "here. The ice is rough at the mouths. After the third one, I'm about a mile. You'll see where the shoreline rises as it goes back toward the mountain, and my cabin's right atop the hill a hundred yards from the river. Trail goes right t' it. I'll have something hot fer ya t' eat and drink when you get there. Take care, now, ya hear?"

Lane and Gabrielle walked Sam across the river ice and watched him disappear into the woods on the other side before they returned to the fire. They had more tea and talked about their plans for breaking camp. Lane said it would be best to pack what gear they needed in the tub. At first light they could store everything else in the plane and start out.

They made a checklist of the items to take including food for two days, the rifle, their clothes, their toiletries, snowshoes, the axe and their survival gear. Lane cross stacked wood on the fire so they'd have hot coals in the morning to build their final fire at the site for cooking breakfast. Then they hit the sack.

A cold, gray dawn beckoned them from their sleeping bags. But the day's expectations outweighed the weather. They eagerly arose and erupted into action. Lane asked Gabrielle, "How'd you sleep?"

"Great, probably the best night's sleep so far."

"Me too."

Lane ran to the outhouse then took down the tarp from the wing while Gabrielle used the facilities. When she reached the fire, Gabrielle volunteered to fold the tarp while he retrieved the outhouse furs. They pulled the horse trough from its storage place under the plane and packed it with their things. Lane tied two wolverine hides hair side down to the bottom of the tub-turned-sled to facilitate smoother travel. Next he tied his parachute cord to a trough handle.

Deciding not to take the remaining moose to Sam's, Lane placed it inside the cargo hold. He told Gabrielle, "I should have thought to send a quarter with Sam, but I'll tell him he can retrieve the moose it he wants to utilize it." He stacked the furs into the plane on top of the moose. Next he set the fuel bucket inside. Their final act before leaving was a good-bye to the camp. Although they were exuberant to be leaving, they shared a mutual sadness knowing their return to civilization would alter the life they'd shared these past four weeks.

As he turned to leave, Lane patted the Beaver's metal skin and said, "Well, *Tundra Bunny,* got to leave you for a while. But I'll be back to get you. Take care of yourself until I do."

Then they were off downriver.

Although pulling the tub was harder than walking solitary on snowshoes, Lane and Gabrielle made fair time, passing the line cabin a few hours out. When Lane figured they were halfway, they stopped for lunch. He built a small fire from dead spruce limbs. In no time, they had hot water from melted snow. They enjoyed a portion of moose each and a celebratory mug up. Before they pushed on, Lane told Gabrielle, "Some of these bush men get weird being alone for stretches of time. It's called 'bushed.' I think Sam is okay, but I just want to let you know to be careful."

Gabrielle thanked him and said, "I'll stay close to you."

Late in the afternoon they passed the first of the three stream mouths Sam had talked about. Just before dark they passed the third. And not much later, as the curtain of darkness lowered around them, they saw artificial light ahead.

Within minutes they were at Sam's. His place looked like a small city on a hill. Lane was puzzled by all the light and wondered how a trapper in the wilderness could have such a set up.

After a month's emotional see-sawing Gabrielle could contain her feelings no longer. As quickly as the realization of rescue dawned on her, she yelled into the wilds, "Lane! We're safe! We're safe!"

"I told you we'd make it. Because we never gave up. Because we made sure we had shelter, heat, food and water. Because we had faith. It was just a matter of time."

Then Gabrielle dropped her snowshoes, lunged toward him, clinging tightly to him, hugging him...wanting to cling to him forever.

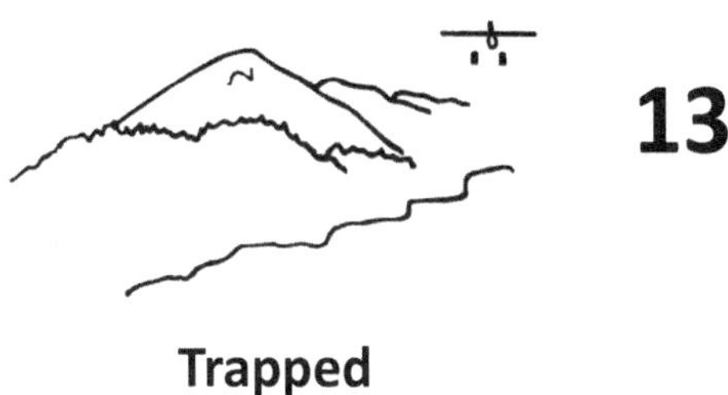

Trapped

Following the trail up the hill to the well-lit cabin was a piece of cake, though the friction on the tub was somewhat telling. Then Lane knocked on the cabin door.

Sam called out, "It's open. Come on in."

Lane and Gabrielle eased inside to a glowing interior. It was more than they could grasp. Although it was a log cabin, the interior sported nearly all the trappings of a city dwelling. They removed their outer gear and boots.

Sam said, "Make yerselves comfortable. I'm choppin' veggies fer a stir fry. But before you eat, you might want t' have a shower t' get refreshed." As an afterthought Sam added, "By the way, I tried t' call out on the radio. Been havin' problems lately. I'll try again tomorra. We'll get you out of here."

Still amazed by his surroundings and wondering where Sam could have gotten vegetables for a stir fry, much less a shower, Lane asked, "So, where did the stir fry veggies come from?"

"Mother Dugan, that's easy," Sam replied, "from my rooty-toot-tootin' root cellar, son. I'm self-sufficient here. I'll explain later. Come on, now, hit the shower. Who's first?"

Although unfamiliar with a trapper's lifestyle but knowledgeable enough to know that most lived on the far side of luxury, Gabrielle spoke, "You're kidding about the shower, right Sam? You don't really have one?"

"Ah, there you're wrong, Dearie. I do have a shower. You don't think I'd have a degree in geological engineering from the U of Doub and live like an uncivilized barbarian, now do you? Geewinikers, no. Right here I got all the amenities of the Hilton. Well, maybe not all the frilly velvety stuff, but enough for any man. I always say, 'If you can't have the best of everything, make the best of everything you have.'"

Lane said, "I considered asking how you did all this, but then I figured we'd find out before we leave." Turning to Gabrielle Lane asked, "Okay, Angel Eyes, want to race me to the shower?"

Gabrielle, having picked up her travel bag and remembering the coin flip at Bret and Mary's house, slowly moved toward the bathroom door. She timed her speech with her movement, "How about if I count to three and we start? One...two..." and as she reached the door, she grabbed the knob and said, "three." Her hazel eyes sparkled, an impish smile crossed her face and she reveled in her act, "Too late. You lose."

Lane knew she'd stolen one of his tricks but took a verbal jab at her anyway, "There you go, pulling a slick New York trick on a country boy."

Sam laughed at their antics and walked toward the bathroom. He pointed out towels, "If you don't like the ones on the towel rack, check the cabinet left of the sink. There's shampoo and conditioner in the cabinet above the sink. I have a big hot water heater and a five hundred gallon water storage tank. Take as long as you'd like."

Thanking Sam, she closed the door, still amazed by the incredible wilderness accommodations. Reveling in the joy of her first opportunity to get thoroughly clean since the forced landing, Gabrielle removed her clothes then slipped behind the shower curtain. She turned on the water until it was as hot as she could stand. She basked in the joy of the scintillating streamlet, absorbing its warmth, while soaking her hair and working the shampoo into a lather.

She recalled earlier horse-trough baths and vowed *never again.* As her body relaxed and warmed with the caress of the water, she allowed herself to fantasize about Lane. About what it would be like being married to him.

She rinsed and shampooed her hair three times. Several minutes passed before she reluctantly left the shower. As she toweled herself dry, Lane's voice interrupted her activity from beyond the door, "Gabrielle, Sam said there's a hair dryer in the cabinet beneath the sink."

"This is too much. A hair dryer out here?" she thought as she opened the cabinet, retrieved the dryer and plugged it in. Blowing her hair she concluded, "This is almost like living in the city." In no time she was dressed, coifed and ready to meet the two hungry men for dinner.

Gabrielle joined them, and Lane whistled appreciatively, "Wow! I knew you were beautiful, but I forgot HOW beautiful!"

Sam added, "Geewinikers, you sure got yourself all gussied up and did it fast."

She blushed, "Thank you, men." Turning to Lane she said, "Now it's your turn."

Lane grabbed his gear bag and disappeared behind the bathroom door. Before long he was back, ready for dinner. Lane had shaved only enough of the whiskers from his face to highlight his red-brown beard, capturing his rugged facial features and framing his gorgeous blue eyes. Gabrielle thought, *What a hunk.* Again, repeating her earlier thought, *I'd like to live with him forever.*

Sam interrupted her thoughts, "Let's eat."

Before them lay a dazzling spread of sparkling China. A veritable smorgasbord covered the table—goblets of grape juice, a pot of steaming coffee, a tray of dried fruit and fresh vegetables, homemade bread fresh from the oven and a ptarmigan stir-fry.

Gabrielle was astonished with Sam's culinary skills and asked, "How did you prepare all this, especially the bread?"

"Home bakin' and cookin' is a hobby of mine. I just rustled up some stuff. I love to cook, partially in memory of Rose. I try a follerin' her recipes. She was a marvelous cook whose specialty was bread and pastry."

Not wanting to forget to tell Sam about the moose quarters in the plane Lane said, "Sam, you're welcome to the moose meat in the plane. I don't know what condition it will be in by the time I get back for the plane. You're welcome to it if you don't mind retrieving it."

Grateful for Lane's offer Sam responded, "Thanks, Lane. I'll get on up there after you leave and bring it to the cabin. I can use it or if you get back to my place, you can take it to Anchorage." Then he warned Gabrielle and Lane, "Since you've been on a restricted diet, you'll probably want t' eat lightly. We can eat slowly all evenin' if you'd like, just so's you don't overeat and get sick."

Gabrielle sighed softly, "Gosh. It's amazing."

Lane asked, "So, how did you happen to come to the bush, Sam? Mind telling us a little about yourself?"

"You might be in for mor'n you want t' hear t'night," Sam began. "I grew up in the Pacific Northwest. Talked t' many who'd come back from Alaska. Was captivated by Alaska's mystique. Decided t' get a degree in engineerin' then head north.

"Got my sheepskin from the University of Washington in '45 when I was 20-years-old. Worked in Anchorage fer three years. Got tired of the rat race and decided t' move out here. Wanted t' enjoy life on my terms...t' have peacefulness and tranquillity of the country life.

"I drew up my idea on paper then set out t' make it happen. 'T'wasn't easy, but I combined prospectin' and trappin' t' add t' my grubstake. Rose and I carved our place out of the wilderness and built the cabin.

"Thought it would be hard on Rose, but she liked it better than I. It was paradise for us out here. She insisted on all the comforts of home too, that's the reason that I have all the woman's finery. I'll stop talkin' fer now so's you can enjoy your meal. If you want t' know more tomorra, I'll tell you then."

Still curious about Sam's scarred face Lane stated, "Don't mean to be rude, Sam, but when you came to our camp, I noticed your face. Couldn't help wondering what happened."

"Oh, that. It's only natural fer folks t' wonder. Mother Dugan, if I didn't run into a skunk bear on my trap line last year. Darned if it didn't turn my face int' the road map yer lookin' at. I was out on the line when a snowstorm hit not long after Rose passed on. Knew I could make my cabin but holed up under a bluff till the snow stopped. Unbeknownst to me the two ptarmigan I carried attracted a wolverine which was a followin' me. Before I knew it, he was jumpin' from atop the bluff onto the birds I'd dropped at my feet.

"Guess he was surprised when he looked up and saw me tucked under the ledge. He jumped at me before I could react. Got a claw stuck in the hole on the closer to my coat zipper and couldn't get it out. Critter like t' tore me apart before I clubbed him loose. He grabbed the birds and skedaddled. I decided I'd better make fer my cabin.

"I managed t' get here through the snowstorm. Stumbled in, turned on the lights, got a mirror, needle and thread and sat down at the table t' begin sewin' them deep cuts. Don't know how many times I passed out, but I finished early the next morning. It wasn't pretty, but it sure worked."

Lane and Gabrielle sat with shocked looks on their faces. Lane said, "You're one tough customer, Sam. That wolverine ruined your day."

Sam chuckled, "You can say that again. Darn near ruined my life."

They finished eating and cleared the table as Sam insisted on filling the dishwasher and putting all the leftovers in the fridge. Then he stated, "I 'magine you folks are pretty tired. Probably be a good idea t' get t' bed and get a fresh start tomorra. Let me show you the guest room. Sorry I don't have an attached bath, but you'll get a good night's sleep anyway on this bed."

Lane explained to Sam, "We brought our sleeping bags, so I'll take mine and sleep on the couch if that's okay"

"Sure thing," Sam said, "if you need anything, just give me a holler."

After "good night" all around they went to their separate quarters.

Gabrielle was saddened to be away from Lane. It was the first night in a month she had not slept bundled up near him. She consoled herself through reflection and writing in her diary.

Awakened by the aroma of frying bacon, eggs and roasting coffee, Lane crawled from his sleeping bag and slid into his pants. He started for the bathroom when Gabrielle noticed him. She couldn't resist a good natured ribbing, "My, my, my, Lane, what disheveled hair you're sporting this fine morning."

He smiled and reiterated her earlier comment to him on the river, "The better to scare you with, my dear. That's how a beautiful lady once responded when I said the same thing to her. If you'll excuse me, I'll remedy my hair." He turned to the bathroom.

When he returned, Gabrielle thought he looked more luscious than ever. He said, "Good morning. Looks like the master chef and his helper have just about got breakfast ready."

"Let's eat. Hope you like sourdough cakes. Got everything ready," the trapper said.

They moved to the table. Mounds of food disappeared while the three visited. Lane began a question, "Sam, last night you talked about your wife, Rose, and designing your home to meet her desires..."

Before Lane could finish, Sam interrupted, "My wife Rose was the light of my life. We had an accident last year, right afore I tangled with the wolverine. She wanted t' go out on the line with me. Somehow she fell through the ice on a beaver pond. I got her out, but it was forty below. Took us two hours t' reach the line cabin just upriver. I got a fire built, thawed out her clothes, got them off her and got her t' bed. We got here a couple of days later, but she got pneumonia. Couldn't save her. She passed on in December. She's restin' behind our cabin on the hillside overlookin' her favorite vista." Sam ran the back of a hand across his eyes.

Gabrielle stole a glance at Lane and they both expressed their sorrow.

Taking the situation into her hands and changing the subject, Gabrielle stated, "It must have been quite a job for you and Rose to gather all these vegetables and feed yourselves."

"You could say all things are relative. We lived off the land. From spring t' fall we collected fiddle neck ferns, mushrooms, berries and raised a garden. We shot moose and small game. I made jerky from some of the meat. We froze and canned some. What salmon we didn't freeze, I smoked or canned. Put in my own water storage tank. Figured out and installed a windmill powered electric system and a backup generator. Bush pilots deliver my supplies. They fly in most of our stuff or contract with someone else to bring in things like the generator and water tank. The river's straight enough fer 'em t' land right out front on floats in the summer, skis in winter."

"It's really amazing what you've done here, Sam," Lane spoke up. "Really amazing. You've made this a comfortable home. Do you miss city life?"

"Tarnation no. This is the life fer me. I don't miss the city, not one bit. In a lot of ways I can't go back t' the city. But in other ways I have the city. For instance, I have such modern conveniences as the internet. You might call me a paradox. I'm like the animals I trap. We both love our freedom. We live one day at a time. The difference, however, is that the fur bearers I trap are in no danger of bein' decimated. But I am.

"I love the wilderness, and Alaska's wildlife is dear to me. But because the food chain includes both predator and prey, some live and some die. We hear criticism about killin' t' eat. Well, I can't photosynthesize food. City folks hunt dead food in cans at the supermarket; I hunt live food in the woods. They may not kill their food, but someone did. We're all hunter-gatherers."

Their leisurely breakfast was evolving into a deep discussion.

Sam continued, "Man has always rubbed shoulders with animals. Explorers sailed the oceans, opened frontiers. The trapper's ocean was the wilderness. Plyin' its rivers and valleys was his voyage into the unknown. All that trappers wanted was a chance t' enjoy their pursuits while garnerin' enough money t' meet their simple needs. Self reliance, individualism, hard work, determination and the hunger fer freedom motivated them.

"The same qualities spawned America. Mountain men, riverboat pilots, cowboys, loggers and prospectors spread American idealism. We opened this country. We were America! Now we're shunned, ridiculed and treated with disrespect to the point of becomin' extinct.

"Geewinikers, I'm a diein' breed, one of the endangered species. I came here in search of personal freedom and t' get away from fellow human predators. T' live among the peaks of God's creation. But those with limited knowledge about man's relationship with animals are tryin' t' end my way of life."

Recalling family memories and wanting to share in Sam's concern, Gabrielle added, "My family was very close and loved the outdoors until my brother's death. I often wonder what my family would be like today had my brother not been shot. It's been very hard for me to accept guns and death caused by them since Gabe died."

Sam responded, "I'm sorry t' learn of yer brother's accident, Gabrielle. Losin' a family member is very difficult. It's also tough losin' pets you love that are a part of your family. I raised three wolf pups after their mother was killed tryin' t' snatch moose meat from a grizzly. She was weakened from givin' birth and couldn't escape the bear. I saved and weaned those little puppies, taught 'em t' hunt. When they reached adulthood, they slunk away t' the wild. Two were killed, but I see the survivor every year or two, either on the trail or peekin' at me from cover around my cabin.

"I named him Whisper when he was a pup. In all his movements he was like a whisper on the wind—as all wolves since time began, he came and went like a shadow on the land. I loved that pup.

Gabrielle asked, "Do you think he'll come back to live with you?"

Sam responded, "Well, Dearie, I'd like his company, but he's a wild thing. Wild things need to stay wild. It wouldn't be right ifn I kept him here.

"One of my jobs was raisin' those pups. Environmentalists and animal rights groups seem t' think they alone will protect our planet. It's not their earth. We're all responsible fer our environment. It falls on all of us t' be good stewards of our earth and its bounty."

Accepting the fact that her views about animals' rights were changing, Gabrielle asked, "How do you respond to strong beliefs about animals' rights?"

Sam answered, "Sincerity in one's beliefs is important. A moose sincerely wantin' t' outrun a grizzly or a wolf pack but losing, is a sincerely dead moose. Some of the things that we sincerely believe or want, happen to be sincerely wrong.

"Animals' rights extremists criticize those doing' the most fer animals.

"Huntin' and trappin' are part of game management. Hunters pay fer licenses, tags, fees and leases which do more fer wildlife than non-hunters. Groups like the North American elk and sheep foundations, Ducks Unlimited and Safari Club International support animals and their habitat. Why, Safari Club donated hundreds of thousands of dollars in Zimbabwe to save the black rhino. And huntin' groups have brought big game back from the brink of extinction to thrivin' levels."

Pressing Sam for more input Gabrielle asked, 'But how do you explain the slaughter of some species?"

"Part of the answer is captured by my friend and fur buyer Gus Gillespie at Alaska Fur Exchange in Anchorage. He says, 'People will pay for the protection of a resource they can utilize.' It's a fact that greed ruled many professional hunters like bison hunters and beaver trappers in the Old West. In Africa, ivory hunters nearly killed off the elephants. Fortunately man reacted in time savin' the beaver and the bison…and so far, the elephant. But we have a responsibility t' learn from others' mistakes and t' prevent its ever happenin' again. There's a sane way t' go about it. Not the extreme measures taken by some.

"Think about those who spike trees or sabotage a hunter's tree stand. What gives them the right t' harm hunters, especially t' the extent of paralyzin' someone fer life?"

Expressing shock, Gabrielle interrupted, "Paralyzed! What do you mean?"

"More than one outdoorsman has fallen from his sabotaged tree stand, sustainin' grievous injury. It's as though we've lost our reasoning powers. Geewinikers, take a look at Oregon and California.

"Because they've closed bear and cougar huntin', totally or partially, there will be more human-predator conflict and more human fatalities. Just wait and see if I'm not right. And there's an irony here. Black bears destroy trees by rippin' the bark off t' get at the inner layer. The extremist animal and environmental groups don't want animals killed nor trees harvested. Yet they corrupt their ideology by tyin' the hands of game management by allowing a thrivin' bear population to kill more trees. Killin' more bears would save more trees."

Still concerned about animals' rights Gabrielle asked, "Where do you see the future of trapping going?"

Sam frowned, "All the complainin' about killin' of the fur bearers is untrue. A trapper won't destroy his income. Proper trapping enhances the game population. Just like a farmer who cares for his land and crops, the trapper is responsible to maintain his fur crop. A case in point, untrapped beavers over-populate and starve."

Lane added, "You make some very strong arguments, Sam."

"Our pilgrim pathfinders planned an America to be proud of. The more our society chips away at our foundation, diluting and destroying our moral fiber, the more damage they do our nation. Unless the citizenry gets a handle on their political candidates and the issues and votes their conscience, we'll continue to see our freedoms eroded.

"Why, our society punishes achievers. Just like the wolf brings down its prey, bureaucrats hamstring producers. Too many do-gooders destroy the good produced by the individual fer the mediocrity of all—we're goin' more socialistic all the time, and divorcin' ourselves of individuality and hard work.

"Look what's happened with welfare. The welfare mentality

impacts lots of people here in Bush Alaska. Although some years furs fetch a handsome price, too many trappers aren't willin' t' expend the energy t' go out on the line. It's easier t' do their trappin' at the post office…waiting fer their welfare checks.

"I s'pose, when it comes right down to it, we're all trapped. You two were trapped on this lonely river, markin' time until you got rescued or until you could rescue yourselves.

"Gabrielle, you're trapped in the evolution of your ideas. Lane's trapped by the conflicts he faces. He wants t' teach in a university, but no such Alaskan university offers his subject, demandin' that he leave this land he loves. He's trapped by his plans. Our society <u>and</u> our country are trapped by erodin' values. That includes everything from abortion t' welfare—we give people money t' have kids whom they abandon. Meanwhile we legalize killin' babies, primarily as a method of birth control. All this time adoptive parents wait years for agencies t' grant them children. I always wonder why extremist groups pour their energies into savin' the plants or animals yet don't vigorously oppose savin' unborn humans."

Lane interjected, "It is disturbing. It's sad that we are subject to those who wish to control us."

"Sure thing," Sam continued, "but the public is mostly to blame. We've given others permission to run our lives. Americans are happy because they've money in their wallets. They kin watch sports or some forgettable TV show. Interest rates are low. The economy's good. But it's time for the silent majority to wake up and become the majority. It's time for us to realize the government isn't our dad. I believe people want the truth. They just need to get some backbone and raise their voices."

"So what you're saying is that it's time for Americans to take our country back?" Lane asked.

Sam replied, "Exactly. Our forefathers paid too dear a price for our freedom. I fought in the war. I've lived long enough to see the disappearin' of America. I'm saddened to see what was once the greatest country in existence go downhill. It may be too late to save this great nation.

"We need less government, not more. My trappin' wild animals pales in comparison t' the government's trappin' us."

Sam's volume rose with his passion, "If it gets much worse, I'm wonderin' if American citizens will take up arms and revolt against the bureaucrats in Washington. If they continue to lead as they have, we may never be able to dig ourselves out from internal destruction or from a foreign take over. Take a strong look at the illegal immigration that's taking place as we speak. And what about the radical Islamic Muslims who have sworn to kill anyone who doesn't embrace their religion? If they want to fit into our society, fine; but they have no right to demand that we fit into theirs."

Lane continued, "The bottom line in all our situations is truth. What is the truth? How do we deal with it? Our situations would be best served if we sought the truth then acted upon it. If people were willing to accept the truth, it wouldn't matter which side you were on. In fact, if we accepted the truth, we'd all be on the same side!"

"Yer, right," Sam concluded. "I'd better try the radio again to see if I can reach Anchorage or somewhere else."

He left for the radio while Gabrielle cleared the table and prepared the dishes for the dishwasher. Lane moved out to the woodpile to split some of the cut logs Sam had stacked against the cabin.

Within a few minutes Sam shouted, "I made radio contact! I told them I'd found the pilot and photo gal. They said they'd send someone out first thing in the mornin'. Then I told them if they didn't know my location t' contact the company that usually hauls stuff out t' me. Looks like your days of relaxin' are over. They'll probably take you straight t' Lake Hood or Providence. And after that...world-wide fame."

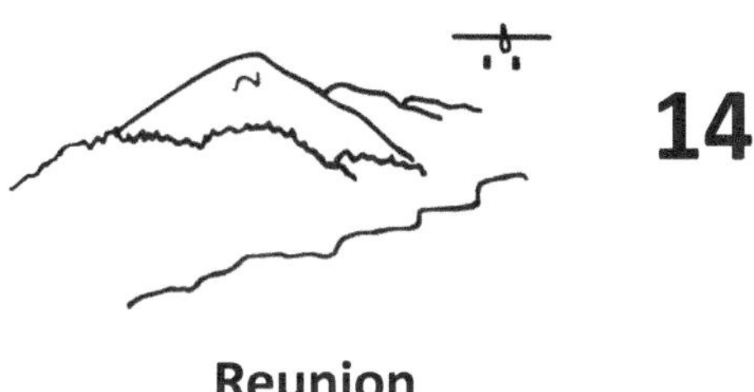

Reunion

The news of Gabrielle and Lane's rescue preceded them. Global media—newspapers, radio, television and even the internet—screamed the headlines: "Bush Pilot Found"; "Pilot and Photographer Pfound"; "Couple Rescued 32 Days Later." It seemed like the whole world prepared for their arrival.

The next morning Gabrielle ran to the window when they heard an airplane engine. Lane and Gabrielle were overjoyed when a Beaver taxied across the ice and stopped at the beach front.

As the pilot left the aircraft and hustled up the trail, Lane recognized his fellow pilot, "Bucky" Starbuck. After hugs and joyous greetings Lane said, "Welcome to Sam's Roadhouse, Bucky. We're mighty glad to see you. This is Sam Mc Callister. Meet Gabrielle. Gabrielle, this is Bucky Starbuck, an Alaskan bush pilot superb and my fellow pilot."

Bucky explained, "You're the talk of Anchor Town."

Sam offered, "Bucky, do you drink coffee? How about some chocolate cake?" Pointing to the table and a chair Sam directed, "Take a load off."

Lane offered, "'Go ahead, Bucky. I'll load up our gear while you're taking a break."

Bucky proclaimed, "Holy Smoke, Sam. If you'd move this set up to Anchorage, I'd be moving in with you. Amazing place you've got here."

Before long they were ready to depart. Lane helped Gabrielle into the passenger seat beside the pilot and he climbed into the cargo compartment. Lane asked Sam if there was anything he could send him from town, and Sam said, "Thanks, Lane, I think I'm okay." They said good-bye to Sam, and then Bucky began his taxi. In moments they were airborne and Anchorage-bound.

Bucky left the Big Susitna River at Talkeetna and lined up with the Big Lake VOR. He called ATIS for weather then contacted Lake Hood approach with intentions. He told the traffic controller his location and that he was inbound over Big Lake. The controller advised him to take the Point McKenzie approach for Lake Hood strip.

In the distance Lane and Gabrielle saw the sprawling buildings of Anchorage. Bucky volunteered, "Looks like we're about there."

They flew over Knik Arm at the boat hull. As he powered over the arm, Bucky checked his carburetor heat. He lowered his flaps for landing and turned final from his base. After touchdown Bucky radioed requesting permission to taxi to AirLaska. When they arrived at their hangar, Bucky and his passengers noticed an ambulance.

Lane's family and Gabrielle's parents were there waiting eagerly for their long lost loved ones. Bucky shut down the bird and they exited to cheers from their well-wishers. Hugging and kissing were the order of the day.

Gabrielle was excited to see her parents. Tears rolled down the cheeks of both her mother and father. Gabrielle wondered how difficult parents' meeting had been for them. Gabrielle's family had left Anchorage when the couple hadn't been found and they had just returned.

After a few minutes a paramedic stepped forward from the ambulance and informed Lane and Gabrielle that he was ready to take them to Anchorage Regional Hospital for physical examinations and treatment. He told them that their families were welcome to follow them and that they could meet in the lobby of the emergency room. All agreed and they left.

In the emergency room lobby the families got caught up on the past month's activities while Lane and Gabrielle waited to be registered.

"It's so good to see you're safe!" Lane's mother said. "To know that our prayers for your safety and return were answered. Even though we trusted your care to God, every day we wondered what had happened and how you were. You look so good. Is that a scar on your forehead?"

Although Lane fully expected to return safely from their situation and knew his family's experience included outdoor adventures of a different nature, he was somewhat surprised by his family's emotional state. He tried to make light of it.

"Yes, mom. I got a little bump. We're glad to be back and in sound condition. I thought about you and the family every day, praying that our ordeal wouldn't be too tough on you."

Trying to include Gabrielle and to downplay the situation, Kelly said, "I wasn't sure when we'd see you again so I bought new Sorels and coveralls. Looks like you'll inherit my old ones, Gabrielle. That will give you an excuse to come back to Alaska."

Gabrielle responded, "I've probably about worn yours out. I planned on buying you new ones anyway. I'm glad you were kind enough to loan them to me. I'm glad I had them; and I'm gladder that I'm back!"

Little Sarah spoke up, "Unca Lane, I sue missed you. My hosey missed you too. Do you tink we could go fo' a hosey wide soon?"

Lane answered, "That would be nice, Sarah. I missed you too."

It was Gabrielle's mother's turn, "Do you think you'll be able to ride so soon?"

Lane replied, "Yes, we're really in good shape. Gabrielle will probably choose horseback as her main mode of travel in the future."

Gwendolyn asked, "Gabrielle, how did you manage for so long?"

Gabrielle responded in such a manner that all within hearing would be privy to her feelings, "Lane told me about a couple who spent 49 days in the Yukon before their rescue. They suffered much more than we. I feel I lived like a queen in the wilderness. I had warmth, shelter, water and food. I even had my personal bath. I feel very fortunate and thankful for Lane's expertise.

"Our situation was less than perfect. But in spite of the lack of proper civilized conveniences, I felt more feminine in the wilderness with Lane than I have in my entire life. I credit all that to Lane's thoughtful care and competence. He saved my life, enhanced my self-esteem and brought immeasurable joy to my life."

Their celebration was interrupted when a nurse arrived to tell Lane and Gabrielle that the doctor was ready to receive them for general physical examinations. She informed the families, "You will be more comfortable in the waiting room, however it will probably be an hour until the doctors complete their exams." The nurse then asked Lane and Gabrielle to accompany her to the emergency room.

Behind individual curtains each put on hospital gowns prior to their examinations. Meanwhile the families politely waited and continued the celebration of their loved ones' safe return.

After the exams the nurse informed them that the doctor would meet with them when they were dressed. They went to the waiting room to await the doctor's arrival. Shortly he arrived and explained his diagnosis. "We've found very little tissue damage to either of you. Your survival skills served you well. You are suffering mainly from weight loss caused by dehydration and a dietary imbalance. We'd like to keep you here a few days to monitor your skin tissue and vitals. It would be best for us to re-hydrate you with proper liquids and re-strengthen you with a strong diet.

"We believe everything will be fine." Having considered their psychological need to remain together and to adjust to people gradually, he continued, "We recommend your sharing a room, and your families will have unlimited access. I strongly recommend you limit the amount of media personnel until you are stronger."

Lane took control, "I appreciate your recommendations. In the interests of our continued improvement, I would like to accept your advice."

Always one to relieve the stress of the moment, Kelly interjected, "Go-ol-ly, Lane, you sure know how to milk the most of a situation. First you land in the woods, now you're taking advantage of the hospital's services and Gabrielle's gullibility." She teased, "Or are you just procrastinating going back to work?"

Lane responded, "I'm not a college grad for nothing. I did learn a few things in school about time management and human relations…." and he added a "you know" for Gabrielle's benefit.

Turning to Gabrielle, he asked, "Angel Eyes, what do you think?"

Gabrielle responded, "I'm in total agreement." She relished the thought that she would be spending more time with Lane. Wanting to see her parents come closer together, she overtured, "Mom and Dad, I'm hoping you'll be able to come see us every day."

Dec looked at Gwendolyn and said, "That would be wonderful. I'm happy to come with your mother if that is what she wishes."

Gwendolyn said, "That will be fine."

Believing that the couple needed rest and that they would be inundated by media people, the visitors decided to leave, promising to drop by the next day.

Expecting media sharks galore, Lane said, "By the way, Gabrielle, we can restrict media people from seeing us if you'd like."

Gabrielle said, "I'm comfortable with your judgment. Although it would be nice to accommodate them with our story and pictures, I expect to sell our story to someone either in part or whole."

Lane said, "Okay, then." He turned to the nurse and said, "We'll accept the first three media calls. Please, hold all other calls for Gabrielle Lacey and Lane Morgan."

Not long after the families' departure local television stations called. Lane invited three to visit them. When they arrived, Gabrielle told them that Lane's piloting skills and expertise in survival saved them. Lane told them, "Gabrielle adjusted to the cold and the hardship extremely well and had a terrific attitude. The Alaska that she came to visit put her to the test, and she passed. Now she'll have more pictures and stories to promote."

The next day a floral delivery driver presented Gabrielle a bouquet of cut flowers and a heavily bowed and wrapped package. While thanking the driver she glanced at Lane, a puzzled look spreading across her face. She audibilized her query, "I wonder who these could be from?"

Lane responded, "No doubt an admirer."

Gabrielle read the note, "To one tough lady. From an impressed observer." She shook her head while saying, "There's no name." Then she turned her attention to the package, tugging at the ribbons. Opening the box, she peeked in and pulled forth a two-foot tall stuffed moose. She smiled and said, "Isn't it cute?"

Gabrielle missed Lane's knowing smile.

Then she noticed the envelope attached to the bull's antlers. She removed the card from the envelope and read,

"Dear Angel Eyes,

       I saw you near the airplane.
       I saw you on the ground.
       I saw you near the campfire.
       I saw you all around.

       We spent a month together
           surviving in the wild.
       That's when I got to know you,
           a special woman-child.

       I hope this moose reminds you
           of things that we've endured
           and when you get discouraged,
           the Son will light your world.

       You're a great and tough lady.
                Your pilot,
                Cowboy"

Gabrielle blushed and thanked him saying, "Lane, you shouldn't have."

He responded, "Oh, yes I should have. I want you to remember our experience and to have good thoughts about it."

A few days later Gabrielle and Lane left the hospital for Lane's. They enjoyed sharing with both families. They read the papers that Lane's family had saved for them—headlines read: "Local Bush Pilot Missing;" "Flight-seeing Photographer Lost;" "No Sign of Missing Aircraft."

During this time both families developed stronger ties. There was much laughter and revelry over the safe return of their loved ones. Gabrielle noticed her parents drawing closer. She was pleased to hear them talk about misunderstanding, forgiveness and strong family ties. It comforted her to observe their good natured behavior and civility toward one another. Much of what Gabrielle noticed confirmed the strong similarity between her father and Lane, a similarity that she'd discovered on the river.

When Lane volunteered to take the Lacey's for a local flight-seeing trip, Dec teased him, "As long as we're not going out in the Bush for an extended stay."

While the four of them flew over Anchorage, her parents kept repeating, "We're so fortunate to have you back, Gabrielle."

They stopped for lunch on their return to Lane's. During the course of the conversation Dec asked the younger couple, "How has your wilderness experience affected you?"

Gabrielle spoke, "You know, I don't think I fully understand yet. I know I'm experiencing a shift in my thinking. But it goes without saying that the experience has changed my life. I'll tell you more when I know more."

Lane added, "I've noticed a number of changes in Gabrielle since I first met her. Maybe it was because we spent all that time together and I got to know the real person. The experience reminded me that we never know what will happen and refocused my understanding that we could die any time."

Ever the philosopher Lane asked the Lacey's, "So, how do you think the experience affected you?"

Dec deferred to Gwendolyn who said, "It opened my eyes. Maybe I wore blinders the past dozen years, but now I see. I realize that things happen, often they are things we can't prevent. I was able to re-evaluate Gabrielle's accident and the assumptions I had made about Gabe. I've made peace with my loss...our loss. And I forgive, maybe where no forgiveness is necessary."

Dec spoke up, "It is wonderful that you and Gabrielle survived the experience. While you were lost, it made us do a lot of thinking. I'm afraid that Gwendolyn, Gabrielle and I all suffered extremely with Gabe's loss. But things happen for a reason. I believe we are all better because of your survival situation. I will continue to be supportive of Gwen and Gabrielle. It has brought Gwen and me closer together. Who knows? Maybe she'll let me move back in with her some day."

His laugh brought laughter from the others.

Gwendolyn added, "Healing is a wonderful thing. I've healed greatly. At this rate Dec and I will probably go on a second honeymoon." Then she laughed.

Remembering their flight Dec volunteered, "I hate to break the mood, but we've got a plane to catch."

Lane said, "Yes, you do. Let's get you to the airport."

They rushed to Lane's and hurriedly loaded the Lacey's things into the family suburban. Gabrielle's parents said good-bye to everyone and thanked the Morgan's. Then they were off to the airport.

Gabrielle hugged and kissed her parents. She told them she would be looking forward to seeing them as soon as she could arrange her schedule.

Dec shook Lane's hand and said, "You've done a great deal for my family. I'll never be able to repay you for bringing Gabrielle and Gwen back."

Gwendolyn hugged Lane and said, "Thank you so much, Lane. You are truly a breath of fresh air. Thank you for taking care of our baby."

Lane responded, "You're welcome." As he winked at Gabrielle, he said, "The pleasure was mine."

Then the Lacey's were off.

On the return to the Morgan's Gabrielle decided if she couldn't have Lane, she didn't want anyone.

Back home Lane walked Gabrielle inside. Wanting to help clean up after the Lacey's departure, he kidded his mother, "It's been a long time since I vacuumed. Let's see if I can remember how."

He finished the vacuuming then took the sheets from the guest bedroom and put them into the washer.

As he finished, Loretta set two banana splits on the table and said to Lane and Gabrielle, "It was thoughtful of you to help me."

Lane teased his mother, "That was the most fun I've had since I changed Sarah's messy diapers." Then his gaze met Gabrielle's and he added, "Well, Angel Eyes, we might as well enjoy our last meal together before you head for home tomorrow."

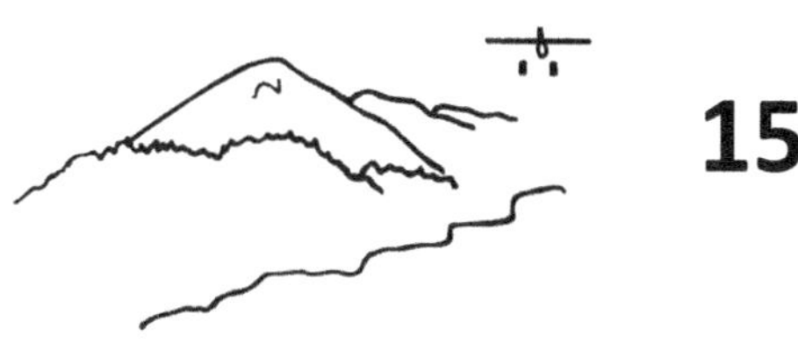

15

Finding the Truth

The next day Lane drove Gabrielle to the airport. Removing her luggage and setting it on the curb, he asked her to wait for him while he parked the car. He returned in a few minutes and helped her check in.

"Gabrielle, your flight seeing turned into quite an adventure. I think you got your money's worth."

"I sure did, Lane." She thought about Lane, his character and person. After five weeks with him, she was having trouble determining how she would deal with leaving him, especially considering her growing love for him. Uncertain of the best response, she added, "More than my money's worth."

Then Lane asked, "You gave me a second chance when I snored; so, when do you s'pose you'll give Alaska another chance?"

Secretly hoping she'd be back to Alaska sooner than later, Gabrielle answered, "I don't know, Lane. I'll see if I can sell our story. You know, I've been contacted by a few national magazines and TV shows. Maybe I can come back up and we can finalize a story or two together."

Lane said, "That would be nice. I'm willing to help if I can." Noting her uneasiness Lane tried to console her, "It will work out, Gabrielle. I hope you have a smooth flight. If your engine quits, at least you'll have more people to enjoy and warmer weather.

"I'd like to compliment you for your attitude during our stay in the wilds. You were a good sport and a fine campmate. I hope you haven't suffered too much for your experience. I look forward to seeing you when next we meet. Until then, I'll be praying for you. Please take care of yoursel..."

Gabrielle interrupted him, "Lane, you've brought a great deal of happiness into my life the past five weeks. I can't thank you enough for that." Stepping toward him she reached out to hug him. At the same time he stepped toward her, threw his arms around her and embraced her.

Wanting to leave him on a happy note and wondering what it would be like to have him return her kiss, she pressed her lips to his and closed her eyes. Lane squeezed her while returning her kiss. It was not a long kiss, but it sent shock waves through her entire body... and his.

When she stepped back, Lane noticed tears running down her cheeks. She turned quickly to walk away and he mimicked her most used phrase, "You know..." then he added his, "you're good to go."

She smiled and cited his flying parlance, "Roger that."

As more tears filled her eyes, Gabrielle walked down the ramp, took her seat and prepared for takeoff.

On the long flight East she played scenes of the last month over and over in her mind. Before she knew it, she'd departed Chicago's O'Hare and was en route to New York's Kennedy International.

Even though Gabrielle wondered if Marcus would be there to meet her, she was not disappointed when he wasn't. His failure to appear only added to her ongoing questions about their relationship. Constant thoughts about Lane and her growing non-interest in Marcus cemented her decision to break their engagement. She would talk to him as soon as possible and return his ring.

In the days to come Gabrielle couldn't get Lane out of her mind. He was a 24-hour closed circuit TV channel with her. When she woke in the morning, she remembered what it was like crawling from under the pile of furs each day with Lane. Before noon she thought of sharing the fire with him. Afternoons caught her thinking about their wood cutting and hauling times. And invariably when she slipped between the sheets at night, she wondered what it would be like to share her bed and her life with him.

Several friends had planned a welcome home party for Gabrielle the following Friday. She was pleased and looked forward to seeing them. By design she arranged to drive early to the party, thinking that she could visit with her good friend Meredith before anyone else arrived. She would then see Marcus for the first time since she'd left; it would be a non-confrontational atmosphere. She could re-evaluate him, even though she had made up her mind about him.

When she arrived, Meredith welcomed her with a warm hug. Although it seemed they'd never been apart, Gabrielle admitted, "A lot of things have changed since I left."

Eager to share with her friend, Meredith used Gabrielle's comment as a springboard, "There have been changes here while you were gone too. Did you know that Marcus and Megan have seen a lot of each other lately?"

Somewhat surprised, Gabrielle replied, "No, I wasn't aware of that. There tends to be truth to the maxim about the cat's being absent and the mice playing. Do you think Marcus and Megan have something going?"

Meredith said, "Gabrielle, I wouldn't do anything to hurt you, but yes. Their seeing each other is more than coincidence. Their relationship is more than they're probably willing to admit to anyone who knows them, and especially to you."

Before long others filled the apartment and their conversations rose to a dull roar.

Marcus finally arrived. Gabrielle saw him and she felt no tingles. He barely acknowledged her. In a condescending manner he kissed Gabrielle's cheek and spoke patronizingly to her. Then he was off to get a drink. That's when Gabrielle noticed his early and constant eye contact with her friend Megan. Marcus' juvenile behavior was duplicated by Megan's, and they stumbled around the room like two love sick moose.

The more she watched Marcus, the more she remembered things about him. He was handsome, smart and arrogant. She also realized that indubitably, Marcus was not the man for her.

She was incensed by Marcus' attitude toward their relationship. However she felt vindicated. She'd found someone better than Marcus. She briefly considered taking her engagement ring off; and announcing to the group that she was giving it to Megan. To her credit, she didn't.

When the last guest had arrived, Meredith asked all to be seated. She began, "I'm sure you all have questions you'd like to ask Gabrielle. I thought she could give us a summary of her experience in Alaska then you could ask her your individual questions."

With that introduction Gabrielle began, "You know, it is wonderful being able to see my friends like this. I want to thank you for the opportunity and for your thinking of me. You might say my trip to Alaska changed my life. What started out as a photo mission turned into a life and death struggle.

"I flew to Nulato, and on my return to Anchorage we had an engine failure. What followed was a month of primitive existence where we had to kill to survive..."

One guest blurted, "You mean, you actually killed something? You can't be serious!"

Somewhat surprised by the rudeness of the interruption, Gabrielle continued, "I've never been more serious in my life. Without that food source, we would have starved. We killed rabbits and a moose. And I shot a bear that was about to attack my pilot..."

Another guest interrupted, "Why didn't you scare the bear away so you wouldn't have to shoot it? Gabrielle, you're not making sense."

Gabrielle went on, "I couldn't have scared the bear. It was either kill it or watch it mutilate my pilot. And it may have chosen me next. I would probably have perished without Lane's help."

Another guest asked, "Why couldn't you have survived on vegetation?"

"The vegetation was under several feet of snow, but we did use some plants that we had access to, like spruce needles.

"I learned a lot about Alaska during the trip. I learned a great deal about myself also. And I learned a lot about life. In spite of our high sounding rhetoric, there's more to life than life. Life would not exist without death. Take our granola bars, for instance. When we eat them, we are eating dead organisms which provide nourishment in some form to our bodies.

"Things in Alaska aren't what we think. There's a vastness to the land and the eco-system that we can't expect to understand from our Ivory Towers in New York. Seeing Alaska up close and personally is different from the emotionalism of non-reality we're constantly subjected to by the metropolitan media."

When Gabrielle realized that her words were going unheard, she questioned the wisdom of continuing. She felt she was wasting her time since her friends chastised her for shooting, for eating meat and for using the furs. And she reprimanded herself, *How can I expect them to understand? It took four weeks in the wilderness for me to get it. And I still don't fully understand.*

She dropped the subject and answered a few questions about her general activities and their rescue.

At evening's end she thanked Meredith again. Before leaving, Gabrielle cornered Marcus. She said, "I appreciate your proposal. I've worn your engagement ring with pride and joy. It's obvious your love for me has greatly diminished in my absence. I have undergone some major changes too, and it doesn't seem practical at this point to pursue our plans together..."

Marcus started to speak, but Gabrielle continued, "It's okay, Marcus. Here's your ring. I wish you the best."

Marcus took the ring without offering an argument, and they parted.

Gabrielle drove to her apartment. Even though the evening was painful, realizing that her friends were fast becoming marginal friends, she was excited on the eve of her trip to Chicago and the taping of a TV show where she and Lane were guests. She would see Lane! Could she wait that long?

As Gabrielle prepared for bed, she rehashed her evening. She picked up her diary and pen from the night stand then pulled back the covers, sat on the edge of the bed, removed her robe and slipped between the sheets.

She opened the diary to her last entry, then penned the following:

Dear Diary,

A new revelation. I can hardly wait to tell Lane. I want to call him now in the worst way, but will try to keep the secret until I see him in Chicago.

The revelation? Life comes from death. Spawning salmon die to provide a food source for the fry when they hatch. As they feed on the dead salmon, the fry turn into fingerlings. Later they repeat the cycle.

Lane talked about Jesus' giving His life for our sins. Doesn't that parallel my analogy about salmon fry? Those who accept Jesus' life and resurrection, have eternal life...and according to Lane, their remaining earthly life is enhanced because they are no longer living for themselves but for Jesus Christ.

Wow!

Lane, where are you! Can I wait to tell you this revelation?

I love you.

Gabrielle placed the diary and pen on her night stand and turned off the lamp. She then audibilized her thoughts, "Jesus, Lane said You are the Way, the Truth and the Life. Wherever you are, I want life. I want my life to be different, like the lives of Lane's family. It's been a long time since I prayed, and I'm not certain of the words. But I know I can be different. Please forgive me for any bad that I've done in my life. Help me to live for You..."

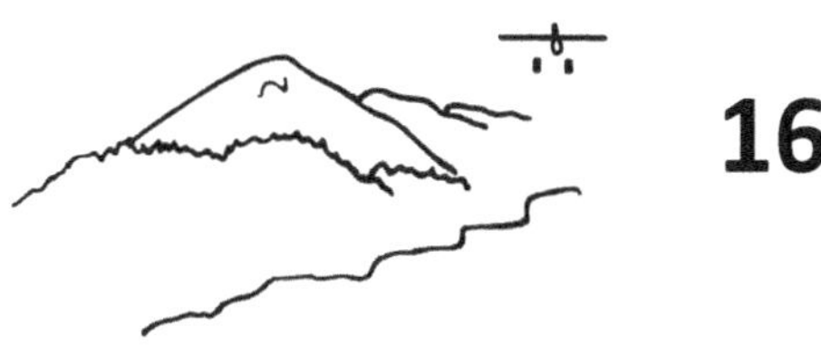

16

Secrets Revealed

Arrangements were made with Great Land Helicopter in Anchorage to transport Lane's Beaver to McGrath where it would be disassembled for return to Anchorage via a large commercial plane. Lane and mechanic Dave Timmons flew to McGrath where the chopper pilot would pick them up. It was a foregone conclusion that they would check the internal structure for damage before trying to sling *Tundra Bunny.* In the interests of expediency and expenses, determining the cause of the engine failure would have to wait until their return to Anchorage.

The chopper's payload required two trips—the first for the Beaver; the second for the men. The whirlybird's pilot explained he was going to make a fuel drop part way to the crash site just in case they needed it for an extra hop.

After they dropped the fuel, they zeroed in on *Tundra Bunny.* The pilot hovered the chopper down beside the Beaver and the men got busy on the ground. While the helicopter crew of the Bell 212 prepared the sling for the Beaver, Lane and Dave examined the plane. He opened the cowling and looked over the engine while Lane walked around the plane.

Dave hollered to Lane, "Looks good, Lane. I don't see anything on the surface that would cause a problem. I'll check the wing spars."

He continued looking while Lane answered, "Okay. I suppose there could be some structural damage. The only damage I see is to the ski and, of course, the wing tip. The prop doesn't appear to be damaged; but you'll probably need to go into the engine anyway."

A while later the helicopter skipper asked, "How's it looking?"

Dave responded, "Structurally it's okay. It's ready to sling whenever you are."

Great Land's people rigged the sling on the Beaver, and the pilot said, "We'll be back for you guys and your cargo as soon as possible."

Lane and Dave covered their ears and watched the artificial blizzard of snow and dust created from the downwash of the chopper's blades. They waved as the tadpole-like chopper rose until the lines were taut on the Beaver. The helicopter pilot's vigilant eyes scanned the horizon then lifted the Beaver five hundred feet before turning toward McGrath. When the rescue machine and Lane's plane were a dot in the distance, Lane turned to Dave and said, "Well, it looks like that little forced landing is going to dent my wallet to the tune of fifteen grand or more. Hopefully my insurance or AirLaska's will cover the bulk of the cost."

In no time the Bell 212 was back. They stowed their cargo and scooted to McGrath where the chopper guys dropped them and their cargo before skedaddling for Anchorage. Lane and Dave disassembled the Beaver for transport.

Two days later at AirLaska, Lane and Dave began work on the Beaver. Lane removed the plane's cargo, stacking the bundles of furs accessibly for shipment to an Outside fur buyer. He made a mental note that he'd also have to drop off the grizzly hide and skull at the Department of Fish and Game and fill out a Defense of Life and Property report, justifying the taking of the animal during a closed season and without proper licensing. Then he went to help Dave.

Lane noticed that Dave had removed the pair of rocker covers. Lane queried, "So, what's up, Oh, mighty mechanic of the North?"

"Pull the prop through a couple of turns." And he watched intently.

"Shouldn't the rocker arms be moving?"

Dave's reply took Lane by surprise, "Affirmative. But the rocker arms aren't rocking, the valves aren't valving, the pushrods aren't pushing, and the pistons aren't..." Dave paused in mid-sentence then stated, "the cam drive gear has broken. Or maybe the cam ring. There's nothing you could have done to discover it during a pre-flight inspection. And there's no way you could have done anything about it in flight!

"In spite of all the effort we put into safety, things happen. Safety and disaster often tread the same paths. Disaster tends to stalk safety, awaiting the opportune moment to pounce. But your skills brought you through a squeaker, Mr. Morgan. Congratulations."

A couple of days later Lane was off to meet Gabrielle in Chicago. On the TV show they were hailed as hero and heroine. When asked how he endured all those weeks, Lane said, "I credit God for looking over us and Gabrielle who took good care of me. We kept warm, had food and weren't injured; so it was just a matter of waiting."

When asked for her response, Gabrielle replied, "This manly Alaska man rescued me...just like the knight in shining armor on the white horse. The main difference between the knight in armor and Lane is that Lane rode a de Havilland Beaver to rescue this maiden in distress."

Since they were staying in the same hotel at the television show's expense, Lane and Gabrielle decided to have dinner together before returning to their rooms. While considering dessert, Lane said, "Well, we survived the wilderness, and so far we've survived the media. We're pretty tough, wouldn't you say?"

Gabrielle said, "Yes, Lane. I'd say we are."

"Lane," she confided, "being back isn't the same for me. Because now I look at life differently. Friends have distanced themselves from me. They don't seem willing to consider the change. It's like if you fail to meet peoples' expectations, they don't approve of you."

"Unfortunately we are judged by others' standards," Lane responded. "When you think about the 'beautiful people,' you see a fawning public. In our search for identity we've elevated celebrities to idol-hood. By outward appearances most celebrities have no sound basis of values. Their wealth-based values make knowing reality difficult for them. Their inability to face reality keeps them from facing life. Their lives are often shallow and self-centered. They follow their own standards. Because of our desire to live vicariously through them, we stoop to their values.

"All too often we fail because we try to meet man's standards. By aiming at man's standards, we target imperfection. On the other hand, God's standard is the real measure of goodness. Think of how parents' relations with their children would be enhanced if those parents followed God's principles. What percentage of parents truly care about and listen to their children? If parents modeled God's love for their children, those children would witness love in action. Consequently they would respect their parents' example and model it.

"A knowledge and practice of Christian principles enables people to be themselves in spite of their humanity because they focus on One greater than themselves. Basing standards on humanness results in a lower level of achievement. Whereas striving to meet the Highest Standard results in a higher and superior standard than man's."

Gabrielle said, "Although new to me in their entirety, I think I understand your comments. My friends can't seem to accept my individuality. They're interested in me only if it benefits them."

Lane said, "I'm sorry, Gabrielle. If friends can't accept you for what you are, they're not really friends. People who know who they are, who are comfortable with themselves, don't need facades and don't need to rely on others' approval for everything they do. They know they don't have to make a show for others. They can apologize when they're wrong. And they don't flaunt themselves or their possessions.

"What about Marcus? Are things okay there?"

"As a matter of fact, no. Well, I guess I should say yes. I broke our engagement. I knew before I left Alaska that things between Marcus and me wouldn't work. And furthermore, he found a new playmate during my absence."

Ever thoughtful and understanding Lane replied, "I'm sorry, Gabrielle. I never met Marcus, but hopefully your loss will be your gain."

Shaking her head in agreement Gabrielle said, "It will."

"So, since you're no longer an on-the-way-to-the-altar-babe, why don't we take in a movie tonight and light up your life?"

Gabrielle could hardly control herself in her excitement. Her eyes sparkled and a huge smile spread across her face as she said, "That would be wonderful." Wanting to tell Lane about her recent decision and about to burst from holding the secret, she added, "But first I have to tell you something."

He looked into her eyes. Ever since he'd first seen her, he loved her dark hazel eyes, alive with adventure and life. That's the reason he called her Angel Eyes. She had the look of an angel, yet those eyes hinted of mischievousness. But now for the first time Lane noticed something he'd never seen in Gabrielle. An excitement and heightened zest radiated from her, complementing her beauty. It lit up her entire countenance.

"Lane," Gabrielle said as she looked into his eyes, "I have a surprise for you. It's the most exciting thing that's ever happened to me." She challenged him, "I bet you can't guess what it is."

Never taking his eyes from hers Lane slid his chair over to her and put his right arm around her shoulders. A growing smile radiated from his face as he lifted her chin with his left hand. Removing his arm from her shoulders, he moved his right hand up her face and smoothed her auburn hair away from her eyes. Looking deep into the eyes he loved, he said, "I'm so happy for you, Gabrielle. I'm pretty sure what you're going to tell me; but I won't rain on your parade. Please, tell me your story."

Gabrielle responded, "Why do you think you know?"

Lane said, "You can't keep that from me. It's written all over your face. No one is ever the same after he invites the Savior into his life."

She leaned forward and pressed her lips to his in a lingering kiss which he returned. "Oh, Lane, I'm so happy. I've never been so happy. I've never known such peace. I'm a changed person."

"That's wonderful. It's okay to change. You don't have to apologize for changing. When did you make your decision?"

Gabrielle told him about the night of her welcome home party, about realizing the connection between death and life in the physical and the spiritual sense. She told him that after she had gone to bed, she asked for God to forgive and change her.

Lane replied, "Congratulations, Gabrielle. You've made the most important decision you'll ever make."

Gabrielle shook her head in agreement and said, "Thank you, Lane. I guess you know it's all your fault. If we hadn't landed on the river, I may have never known."

Lane responded, "In that case, it's a wonderful blessing that we lost an engine and landed on the river."

Eyes still sparkling, Gabrielle added, "Oh. Guess what? You've been calling me Angel Eyes all along. I have another secret I never told you."

"Oh, yeah, what's that?" Lane asked.

She responded, "When my brother was born, my parents named him for the angel Gabriel who visited Mary. God told Mary she would deliver the Son of God. They weren't expecting me. But when I came along a few minutes later, they decided an appropriate name for me would be Gabrielle."

Lane said, "Well, how about that! I had good reason to call you Angel Eyes all along. You were named for one and you are one! Let's go celebrate with that movie."

On their way to the movie, Lane thought about their discussion on the river about prospective spouses. He realized more than ever that perhaps Gabrielle was capable of filling his long-formulated check list. He pondered his comment to her that it was okay to change. Obviously he, too, was undergoing change.

He wanted a woman to share his faith.

He wanted one who would be faithful to him, and only time can test faithfulness.

He had no doubt about her personality…she got an "A" there.

The only way to test for motherliness was by observing her around children. He'd been impressed by her relationship with his niece Sarah.

He'd struggled with his idealistic view versus God's realistic view of things that man doesn't see. Lane recalled his comments about people's inability to recognize reality, and thought "Maybe I'm learning a lesson in change, a change from my idealistic list to God's realistic one."

After the movie they returned to their hotel. Knowing they would be going their separate ways the next day, Lane suggested they stop at the hotel restaurant for a snack. Lane agreed with Gabrielle that sharing a giant banana split would be a great way to end the evening.

Although Gabrielle's evening was one of the best in her life, she wasn't saying much. Lane picked up on this and said, "Okay, Angel Eyes, so what's on your mind?"

She told him that she was feeling alone since her friends were giving her the cold shoulder. She said, "I'm waiting for my film to be developed and to see what happens with our story. I queried a couple of magazines." Inwardly she longed to return to Alaska to be with Lane. "I'm finding little challenge in New York, other than dodging taxi cabs."

Wanting to help her feel better and wondering if her return to Alaska would answer his questions…and perhaps hers, Lane said, "So what's to stop you from a visit to Alaska? You could throw your sleeping bag on the floor at our place. If you want to re-live your experience on the river, you could spend the night inside the local cold storage freezer."

Gabrielle's eyes lit up and she nearly shouted as she scooted around the table. She grabbed Lane's hands and asked, "Do you mean it, Lane?"

Surprised by her excited response, Lane said, "Of course, Gabrielle. You know I always say what I mean and mean what I say…"

"Oh, Lane," Gabrielle sighed, "that would be wonderful. But what would your family say? Do you think they'd mind?"

Lane responded, "Gabrielle, you know my family well enough by now to know that they would enjoy having you…as long as you don't ask Kelly to borrow her coveralls for a flight to Nulato."

Gabrielle squeezed his arm and kissed him on the cheek. "You're on. When can I come?"

Lane answered, "What's wrong with tomorrow? You grab some gear and we'll travel together. We could go to your apartment in New York and schedule a flight from there."

They finished their snack and Lane walked Gabrielle to her room. She clasped his arm in hers and slightly pressed her body against it as they walked. In ecstasy she thought *I'll be with Lane in Alaska. We'll never part again.* She was so excited her body seemed to float above the floor.

At her door Lane said, "Thank you for the wonderful evening. You have crossed a great chasm. I'm looking forward to seeing you tomorrow." With his arms around her and his hands pressing gently against the small of her back, he eased her toward him, leaned over and kissed her ever so lightly on the lips.

Gabrielle sighed, "Thank you, Lane for the evening…for caring." Then she turned and disappeared behind her door. She called and arranged for air travel to Alaska.

The next morning promptly at 8:00 a.m., Lane carried his suitcase to Gabrielle's room. He knocked on her door. Gabrielle invited him in and he helped her snap her suitcase closed. He picked up her grip and grabbed his as they left her room. Next they went to the restaurant for breakfast. From there they took a taxi to the airport and left for

New York.

Taking a cab to her apartment, Gabrielle hurriedly threw together some clothes and she and Lane returned to the airport where they left in due time for Anchorage.

Gabrielle enjoyed a grand reunion with Lane's family. It was almost as though she'd never left. One night she and Lane drove to an overview on Upper Huffman to see the lights of the city. They even went for a night flight in the restored *Tundra Bunny* and Lane pointed out different sites.

One day Lane asked Gabrielle if she'd like to go horseback riding, "Remember I promised Sarah I'd go riding? How about all three of us going?" Gabrielle thought it would be a wonderful idea, so Lane picked up Sarah and brought her to his house. The three went to the barn and prepared for the ride.

In the barn Lane grabbed a halter and lead line and secured Banjo, his mother's horse. When Gabrielle asked him the history of the horse's name, Lane answered, "Dad has always wanted to learn to play the banjo. I suspect mom named the horse Banjo to help dad keep his dream alive."

Then he grabbed the body brush and hoof pick and returned to the horse. As he picked each hoof and scraped away debris, he talked to Sarah about the importance of checking hooves for rocks and cracks and to make sure the shoes were tight.

He picked the hooves and brushed each horse before blanketing, saddling and bridling them. Then he led them to the yard and tied each to the paddock fence. As soon as all three were together, he helped Gabrielle onto Lightning, Kelly's aptly named horse—because it was so slow!

Lane helped secure Sarah's helmet then placed her on her horse Precious and said, "You have a nice daddy, Sarah. He was thoughtful to trailer your horse here so we could ride together. Be sure to hold tightly on the reins while you hold a handful of mane in your other hand. Tell Uncle Lane if you need something, okay?"

Sarah said, "Okay, Unca Lane."

They rode the familiar gravel road to a nearby trail then spent an hour enjoying the horses, the ride and the woods in the Chugach foothills before turning for home.

As soon as they reached the barn, Lane said to his companions, "Well, we didn't ride off into the sunset, but we had a good time didn't we?"

Although Sarah was too young to understand the "sunset" comment, she shook her head up and down and Gabrielle responded affirmatively.

Lane helped Gabrielle down off Lightning and together they

helped Sarah. Gabrielle held the two horses while Lane led Banjo to his paddock. Then Lane put the other horses in their paddocks, secured the gates and carried the saddles, bridles and blankets to the barn. He told Gabrielle and Sarah, "Now we need to brush the horses and make sure they're recovered before we leave them. We can leave Precious here until your daddy can come get her."

He let Sarah help grain and hay the steeds while Gabrielle started brushing them. While the horses ate, Lane checked each one's hooves.

At dinner that evening Lane said, "I think it's about time to take Gabrielle on a clamming caper. After all, she needs a few more Alaskan experiences to add to her photo portfolio. What do you think?"

Everyone agreed. Park said, "Clam tides are good for several days starting day after tomorrow. We can pack up the old suburban and take off in the middle of the week to avoid the masses of clam smashers."

Loretta added, "Why don't we check with Ginger to see if they can go. Brad may be able to schedule his work so he can go along."

Park replied, "Good idea."

Lane volunteered, "I'll gather up the shovels, buckets and coolers and grab a couple of .22's for some target shooting along the way. Mom, I'll help with sandwiches."

Gabrielle offered, "Please let me know what I can do. I want to help as much as I can."

Loretta thanked Lane and Gabrielle and asked Kelly if she'd mind rounding up their favorite 50's and 60's music cassettes for the trip and calling to ask Ginger if she'd bring her video camera and some desserts.

Then Lane said, "We'll give Gabrielle something to remember about the wild and crazy Morgan outings."

Gabrielle chimed in, "I think I already have a pretty good feel for the Morgan outings based on one particular flying experience."

And they all laughed.

A few days later on their return from clamming Gabrielle said, "When we started, I thought we'd be using those long handled nets for clams."

Lane restrained laughter, smiled and responded, "As you discovered, those nets aren't for clams. When we get back to Portage, I have something to show you."

In an hour Lane pulled off the roadway onto the shoulder just a few miles west of Twenty Mile River. Then he said, "Okay, everybody out. We're going fishing for candle fish." He opened Gabrielle's passenger door and helped her and Sarah out. Then he grabbed two nets and took Sarah's hand, "I'll help my favorite niece across the highway." Looking back he saw his parents and sister exiting the suburban. Then he called to Gabrielle, "Come on, Angel Eyes."

Gabrielle ran across the Seward Highway and scooted over the guardrail with Lane and Sarah. Lane handed Gabrielle a net and said, "I'm going to help Sarah try to catch a hooligan. You can try too."

Lane helped Sarah hold the 10-foot handle, dropped it into the brown, silty water of Turnagain Arm and slowly swept it downstream with the current. They felt a bump and pulled the net to shore. Lane dumped two wiggley, 10-inch fish onto the ground.

In no time Gabrielle shrieked, "I've got one!" She hauled her net from the water and discovered three hooligan.

By then the others had arrived with more nets and a couple of five gallon buckets. Lane put the fish into a bucket while watching the others fish, laughing at Sarah and Gabrielle who tried to get as close to the water without getting splashed by periodic waves.

Gabrielle was overjoyed, "This is so much fun." Her next statement was a question, "I assume these little critters are good to eat?"

Lane responded, "Some say yes; some say no. We do this every year and enjoy eating them."

Loretta added, "At least Lane does. The rest of the family is pretty burned out on hooligan."

They fished another hour while the tide continued to drop. They'd caught a couple of hundred hooligan when Loretta said, "I think we have enough fish to clean for a while."

And Park added, "True. Let's head for the barn."

A week after their return Lane took Gabrielle out for dinner at The Regal Alaskan where he told her, "It's fitting that I bring you here where Your Royal Highness may enjoy your just desserts. Mind you, we're not eating just dessert, but I think you'll enjoy the atmosphere, the view, planes landing and departing Lake Hood, the cuisine and the service. And, of course," he teased, "your manly-man escort."

By this time she had decided she wanted to live in Alaska and share its lifestyle with this wonderful man. While eating Gabrielle said, "Remember when we saw the video at Bret and Mary's? The reason I was crying isn't because I was sad. I was sad because Lucy fell in love with someone other than her unconscious 'fiancé.' I was wondering if the same thing was happening to me. If I was falling in love with you, my tears were not for Marcus—they were for me. I was crying because I didn't want to make a mistake by marrying the wrong man."

Somewhat reticent, but knowing that she had to get it out of her system, she told him what she'd wanted to for weeks, "I'm interested in continuing our communication and working on our long term relationship."

He replied, "Let me see if I've got this right. You're wondering if you can be more permanently involved in my life?"

Gabrielle said, "Yes. I know that we haven't known each other very long, but..."

Lane interrupted, "Sometimes time is unimportant when one knows in her heart what she wants. Knowing you as I do, I'm certain you know what you want from our relationship."

Pleased with his response, Gabrielle responded, "Yes, I do. You know, I'd like a permanent relationship. As in the "m" word. "M" for matrimony."

Lane queried, "You mean as in 'I be the pilot; you be the co-pilot'?"

Gabrielle responded, "Affirmative. As in you be the daddy; I be the mommy." If you say 'no,' she smiled and called forth one of his favorite phrases, "it could ruin my whole life."

With a smile on his face Lane replied, "New York Tower, this is Beaver one-niner-six-niner Bravo, inbound. Request complete stop. Intentions to cover your entire airport with hugs, kisses and much more...forevermore."

Gabrielle's smile glowed. She threw her arms around him in a bear hug and shrieked, "New York Tower to six-niner Bravo, I'm good to go!"

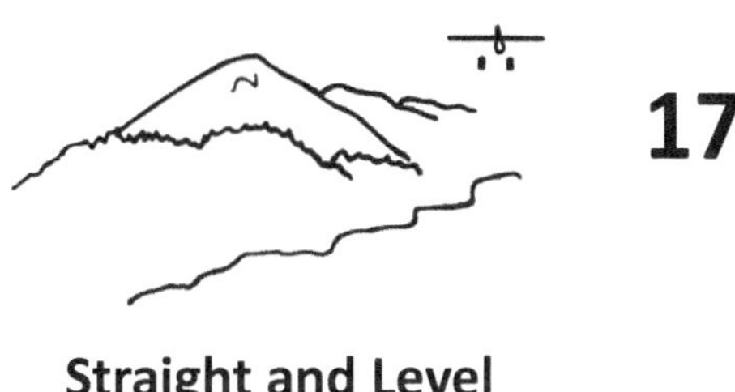

17

Straight and Level

Gabrielle and Lane decided on a June wedding in Alaska. They agreed that her real friends were in Alaska. Lane teased her, suggesting that they honeymoon in Nulato, "After all," he said, "that's how this whole thing started." He told her that it would be good to see their Nulato friends Bret and Mary at the wedding.

That night Gabrielle received a call from her mother. Surprised, Gabrielle said, "Mother, I was going to call you tonight."

Gwendolyn said, "I guess I saved you a dime. I just wanted to let you know that your father and I are making giant strides. The chances of our getting back together are growing daily. He called me again today to tell me that he's never stopped loving me. As hard as it's been over the past twelve years, I told him I felt the same way. Since you've always wanted us together, I just thought you'd like to know." Her mother paused a moment then asked, "And then, guess what?"

Gabrielle couldn't guess so her mother continued, "I received a dozen long stemmed red roses just after he hung up. I think he's courting me, the old dog."

Gabrielle said, "Mother, shame on you referring to dad as a dog..."

Gwendolyn interrupted, "I always called him that as a term of endearment when we were together."

Gabrielle continued, "He probably figured the flowers were a reminder that he never has stopped loving you." Gabrielle was thrilled with the news and thanked her mother while wishing her the best. Then she continued, "Mother, I have something to ask you. Would you be interested in coming to Alaska for the third time in three months? Lane and I are getting married, and we'd love to have you and dad here. What do you think?"

Gwendolyn squealed, "Oh, Gabrielle! Congratulations. I'm so

happy for you. I kind of expected it. You and Lane were getting along so well. Just give me the details. Do you want to call your father or do you want me to?"

Gabrielle responded, "I'd love to have you call him, mother. Are you going to invite him on your second honeymoon, or will you wait for him to invite you?"

Gwendolyn said, "Basically the ball's in his court. I know he'll make the right decision."

"Okay, mother. Gotta go. I have lots of planning to do for the wedding. It's June 5, your birthday. I'll keep you posted. I love you."

Gwendolyn replied, "Bye, Dear. I love you too."

Gabrielle hung up and told Lane, "Lane, that was my mother. She said that you literally transported me across the state of Alaska; and she's glad that you're transporting me to the state of holy matrimony.

"It's interesting that the emotional distance between my parents and me as well as the distance between my mother and father is changing. I'm becoming closer to them, and they're drawing closer to each other. Isn't that what happens when God confronts us? Our distance from Him is reduced."

Lane said, "Yes, Gabrielle. God always tries to reduce the distance between Him and us. I'm glad your parents are doing so well. It will be fun seeing them again."

Gabrielle pointed out, "On a related note. You transported me from a spiritual wilderness full of doubts and uncertainties into a haven of rest, into the waiting arms of Jesus Christ. I'm so thankful, Lane."

Lane smiled and squeezed Gabrielle's hands, "That makes two of us, Angel Eyes."

Gabrielle continued planning the wedding as Lane supported her and reminded her that everything would work out well. They met with the Morgan's pastor Dale Steele for marital counseling.

Knowing that Kelly enjoyed making cakes for special occasions, Gabrielle asked her to make theirs and to assist with her expertise. They made a great team—Gabrielle appreciated Kelly's input; and Kelly was overjoyed that she could help and that her brother was marrying such a wonderful woman.

Kelly took Gabrielle to the local flower store and selected flowers and greens. Gabrielle wanted a non-traditional arrangement. She wanted it to be striking yet simple. She chose burgundy cymbidium orchids, white dendrobiums and several other exotic flowers and greens.

She planned on having high style centerpieces for the tables at the reception. She ordered two large pieces, several small arrangements for the guest book table and reception room and candelabras for the front of the church.

Gabrielle and Lane had talked about their favorite cake flavors and decided on traditional white cake with raspberry filling, a four-tiered affair with fresh flowers on each layer. The flowers all matched the orchids and greens in her bouquet. They picked tasteful corsages and boutonnieres for parents, grandparents and special guests.

Gabrielle selected a V-necked wedding gown with long sleeves and a beaded bodice. Beautiful lace covered the gown and its six-foot train. While modeling her gown, Lane's Angel Eyes was as regal as a queen.

Lane would wear a charcoal double breasted tuxedo that complimented his statuesque physique.

Lane wanted to surprise his bride and asked Kelly to make a special vase arrangement of roses and stargazer lilies which would be delivered to the hotel's honeymoon suite the night of the wedding. He wrote a special card telling Gabrielle how much her cowboy sky-jockey loved her and how hard he would try to meet her expectations and to make her happy. In part it read, "My hope for our decades of married life is that they will be straight and level. I'll do whatever it takes to keep the aircraft of marriage aloft. Though there may be contaminated fuel, wind sheers and what not, I'll be at the yoke flying my very best."

In early June Dec and Gwendolyn arrived at the Morgan home, adding to the festive and normally active atmosphere. The Lacey's arrival was a happy reunion all around. Their presence filled the home almost to bursting. Fortunately the barn housed two guest rooms—a person merely needed to negotiate around Park's crated Beaver in order to get to either room.

The day before the wedding Lane flew to Sam Mc Callister's cabin. Gabrielle and Lane had invited him to the wedding, and he'd gladly accepted. The families met Sam and extended their gratitude to the trapper.

On the big day the wedding families and Sam shared a monster breakfast in family fun and enthusiasm, laughing and having a good time. They'd gotten along like best friends the entire time. After breakfast they erupted into action, targeting final activities before the evening affair.

When the joyous hour arrived, the families were in attendance with an elevated level of excitement. Family and friends waited in expectation while bridesmaids and groomsmen prepared in their separate dressing rooms with the bride and groom. The women chattered in their excitement, complimenting Gabrielle on how beautiful she looked in her wedding dress. They asked the normal "how does my hair look?" and "would you help me with my dress?" questions. Meanwhile the men joked and teased Lane, most were childhood freinds. The wedding party was happy for this special couple.

Before they knew it, the guests had taken their seats in the church and the ceremony was underway.

Lane and his groomsmen waited. The beautiful bridesmaids' movements matched the keyboard's legato and largo—smooth and flowing, slowly and in a grand manner the beauty of the maids, blossom by blossom, filled the aisle with spring. And as the reverberating notes from the piano began the finale, the bride appeared, loveliest of all.

When the wedding march began and Gabrielle flowed down the aisle in unison with her father, Lane thought about their short courtship. He was excited for his new life with Gabrielle and knew he had made the right decision. He felt that her radiance filled the sanctuary. As the thought that he'd never seen her so captivating entered his mind, he realized that he was about to begin one of the most critical relationships of his life, and he vowed to give his all to the accomplishment of a loving husband.

The ceremony went as rehearsed until just before the exchanging of the rings. Ever full of surprises, Lane left his bride-to-be and walked toward the piano. When he was within ten feet of the instrument, the pianist rose as per Lane's secret, previous arrangement and took a seat nearby. The wedding party, parents and pastor, mouths agape, stared in obvious surprise.

Lane sat at the piano and fingered the keys. He played the introduction to the song he had arranged for his bride and announced, "This song is for my true love. I've named it 'Truly You' in your honor, Gabrielle." As he began the melody, he sang of her beauty in body and spirit. Then he sang of his pledged fidelity to her. He completed his song then returned to the altar. He winked at her and observed obvious tears of joy flowing down Gabrielle's cheeks.

The song reminded them of the depth of their love for each other. Though theirs was not a traditional long term dating relationship, both Lane and Gabrielle knew theirs was a love no one could take away.

After the rings were exchanged, the minister said the words that so many had awaited, "You may kiss the bride." Lane gently lifted Gabrielle's veil. Their eyes met. There was a momentary pause. Lane leaned forward as did Gabrielle. Their lips met and Lane bent Gabrielle back at the waist while she wrestled to keep her veil on. A loud cheer of approval rose from the well-wishers. Lane leaned Gabrielle erect and they clasped hands.

Lane and Gabrielle turned to face their supporters. Then Pastor Steele announced, "It gives me great pleasure to introduce Mr. and Mrs. Lane Morgan." Jubilant clapping, cheering and whistles filled the air.

As Lane led his new bride down the aisle to the reception,

Gabrielle said, "I didn't know you played. On second thought, I didn't know you sang."

Lane replied, "I'm just full of surprises, Mrs. Morgan. I'll save one for you for each year of our seventy-five years of marriage."

After the reception the new Mr. and Mrs. Lane Morgan stepped into a horse drawn carriage with their parents and took a leisurely but brief ride around the neighborhood. Gabrielle expressed surprise at the conveyance, and Lane told her, "I wanted to surprise you. I asked Ginger to make the arrangements. She's our family horse person and has the connections."

When they returned, they discovered that friends had performed the traditional car decorations on their vehicle, including a number of five gallon cans tied to the bumper. Lane helped his wife into the balloon filled car then started toward their future, waving to friends.

A chivaree ensued with several vehicles following the newlyweds. They ended up at Lake Hood. Lane helped their parents and Kelly into his Beaver. They taxied for take off and were followed by thirty well wishers in seven small aircraft.

Lane led the group amidst good natured radio banter over the Anchorage landscape then up the Knik River. As they flew over Knik Glacier, Lane told Gabrielle, "Although that's a big chunk of cold down there, I will never be cold to you. As a glacier is continually on the move, so will be my love for you, constantly growing. I will reach out to you, moving through obstacles to build a strong and enduring relationship with you."

Gabrielle blushed, "Oh, Lane. How sweet. You set a very high standard which I will try to meet." Then she leaned over and kissed her husband on the cheek.

He teased, "Don't distract your pilot. I'm having enough trouble keeping my mind on my job as it is."

Before long they were back at Lake Hood and de-planed. The couple bade their final good-byes before heading to their hotel. Lane had reserved the honeymoon suite at the Captain Cook Hotel in town, planning to spend the night and leave the next day for a honeymoon in the Swiss Alps. On their way to the airport they would stop by his home for their luggage.

By the time they reached the hotel, it was nearly midnight. Lane carried their luggage to their room where he opened the door. Then he picked Gabrielle up and carried her over the threshold. He set her down and they threw their arms around each other. Looking into each other's eyes they simultaneously said, "I love you." Their lips met and a lingering, passionate kiss sealed their commitment.

Lane set their suitcase inside and locked the door. He suggested they watch the sunset while snuggling on the couch.

Gabrielle excitedly shrieked when she saw the flower arrangement.

While reading his card, she swooned and told Lane how thoughtful he was and how much she loved him. She said, "I want to be the best wife you could ever hope for."

He responded, "I'm sure you will be."

Lane led her to the couch, and moments later as the red-orange orb dropped behind the Alaska Range, Gabrielle kissed Lane's neck as her fingers toyed with his hair. He gently ran his hands over her back.

Gabrielle said, "You know, Lane...there's a parallel between Nulato and New York. The Big Apple has lottos, but nothing like Nulato. You're my Nulato grand prize...my New Lotto!"

He kissed her cheek and thanked her, "That's mighty nice of you to say."

Then she asked, "Remember after I shot the bear and you held me in your arms? You said, 'That's got to be the most exciting bath you'll ever take!' You know, you were wrong. Guess what? The hot tub in our suite will witness my most exciting bath ever!"

Teasing her, he mussed her hair and mimicked her, "You know, your hair is disheveled. And, here came his John Wayne imitation, "Missy, when you asked me to marry you, I forgot to tell you...I'm allergic to water."

Gabrielle jumped on him and started tickling him while saying, "Oh, no you don't, Cowboy. I know you better than that. You're good to go."

Books by Larry Kaniut

Alaska Bear Tales

Instant Sourdough

More Alaska Bear Tales

Cheating Death

Some Bears Kill

Danger Stalks the Land

Bear Tales for the Ages

Alaska's Fun Bears

Alaska Air Tales

Brachan

Trapped

SAFE with Bears (Stay Alive From Encounters)

Alaska Bear Tales

Comprehensive research about man-bear encounters includes victim, rescuer, family and medical comments—from false charges to fatalities.

I was lucky enough to have Mr. Kaniut as an English Teacher around 1980. During that time he read us stories from *Alaska Bear Tales*. As a struggling student he made me want to read and write. Mr. Kaniut does a great job in pulling the reader into the story. His ability to get people to share the most horrific details of their encounters with bears keeps you wanting more.

Anyone looking to read real life drama this is the book to start with. You will not want to put the book down.

Amazon reader, Daniel Bird, Seattle, WA, November 12, 2000

Instant Sourdough

Humorous definitions of Alaska terminology, most of which goes over the head of Cheechakoes (or newcomers)…words like Spenard divorce and bear insurance.

More
Alaska Bear Tales

Many bear stories with greater emphasis upon humor than original book.

Great Book and Fast Read. Spine tingling reading full of chills, thrills, and even some laughs. Do not pass this book up but be prepared to not be able to put this book down!

Reviewer from San Luis Obispo, CA August 12, 1999

An eye opener…much more than a blood and guts thriller. It affords the reader an open minded look at the attacks and as you read you find yourself second guessing the victims. Larry has put forth alot of effort in his research. I enjoyed the book and hope that there is a book three in the works...

--Reviewer: jdmiles@worldnet.att.net from Arizona

October 28, 1998

Cheating Death

Eighteen stories of outdoor mishap in Alaska.

"I was not able to put it down. You have that rare gift which transports a reader and immerses him into the story so that he actually feels the emotions of the minute. Possibly you are the PAGEMASTER."

--P.K. Willis

"I have enjoyed *Cheating Death*; the story about Mike Harbaugh is terrific, reminding me of my close calls in similar flying conditions. All your stories are good reading."

--Lowell Thomas, Jr., former Lieutenant Governor, State of Alaska

After my 2 trips to Alaska (3 months RV, and then a cruise) I really enjoyed reading this book and discovering even deeper the wild and dangerous side of Alaska. Kept me reading, and was hard to put down. I finished reading the book in 2 days and shared it with my neighbors. I actually went on the Boat Adventure from Talkeetna, AK, as we were in the class 4 rapids - the owner went further - as it describes in the book, and after meeting him, this inspired me to buy the book.

5.0 out of 5 stars Amazon reader, Loretta Savary, January 12, 2010

… "one savors the triumph and giddiness of survival when survival seems out of the question."

--General Aviation News & Flyer

Some Bears Kill

Thirty-eight stories involving men struggling against the hairy, four-legged beast known as bear.

Three of the best known writers about Alaska are Rex Beach, Jack London, and Robert Service…All of those authors are from a period, early in this century, when Alaska was a vast, unknown territory. Their stories and poetry helped in formulating a vision, often inaccurate, of Alaska that continues to this day in the minds of armchair adventurers. Larry Kaniut is destined to join Beach, London, and Service as one of the best of Alaskan writers.

--Wayne Ross, attorney at law, National Rifle Association
past vice-president

Danger
Stalks the Land

Forty-two stories ranging from saltwater to mountaintop…pitting man against the nasty elements dished out by Mother Alaska.

Good book for city slicker youth, say 14 years old and up. As opposed to video games or TV, reality just oozes from every Pg. Not a bad thing to hammer home the actions/consequences theme in a young'un, Lord knows Darwin isn't welcome in modern society.

Amazon reader Michael Eckhardt, 5.0 out of 5 stars **Amazing stories**, March 11, 2010, (Douglas, AK)

Mind numbing true adventure! 5 stars This is easily the best collection of true adventure tales ever assembled. I was blown away by the courage, danger, and pure adrenaline running through these stories. My advice: run to your nearest bookstore and BUY THIS BOOK!

--Jim Walters (jimwalters@regency.org) Washington State, Nov. 19, 1999

A pair of youthful newlyweds embarks on a gold-panning outing, but only one returns alive. Twelve climbers, roped together in groups of four, plunge down a mountainside, landing in a twisted heap of mangled bodies. A geologist on a mapping expedition radios to her superiors: "I'm being eaten by a bear!" These are just some of the vividly rendered disasters and close calls Alaskan writer Kanuit details in this collection of true life adventures. Stretching from the mid-19th century to the recent past, the 43 pieces are plenty scary, but Kanuit, a former high school teacher who has lived in Alaska since 1966, also uses the stories to teach valuable lessons about character, loyalty and courage. In some cases, the difference between survival and death is no more than happenstance. But in others, disaster is due to inexperience or the failure to recognize a dangerous situation. Short introductions and brief teasers leading to the next story help move the reader through the book, and an appendix contains valuable information on what it takes to have a chance of survival in the Alaskan wilderness.

Publishers Weekly

Your book has jumped to the front of my reading list, the other twenty books under the bed will have to wait a couple of days til "danger" is finished. One day into the book and half of it read already. Eagerly awaiting your next book. Cheers Andy

email - Andy Millard, South Wales, UK, November 11, 1999

THE ULTIMATE HUMAN TRIUMPHS AND TRAGEDIES   5 stars

READING THESE REAL LIFE ACCOUNTS WILL LEAVE YOU MARVELING AT THE POWER OF THE HUMAN SPIRIT AND THE WILL POWER SOME MEN HAVE TO LIVE. YOU WILL SEE HOW TRAGEDY CAN STRIKE

Mr. Kaniut. Thank you for your publication *"Danger Stalks the Land."* There are several things I appreciated most, 1-The articles and stories were more recent, 2-The bystanders and survivors were able to look back and capture what they might have done differently 'next time.' As an active Board Member and active field member of Pacific Northwest Search and Rescue and a Survival Instructor at (NWSOS) Northwest School of Survival, I am always looking for examples, results, and follow-up on searches and rescues. I am also the editor of our SAR groups monthly newsletter. I hope you don't mind, but I took the liberty of recommending your book to our group! Thank you! If you are ever in Clackamas County, feel free to stop by one of our monthly meetings. We'd love to hear your experiences. Thanks you for this opportunity.

Hello and thank you for doing such a great job with my dad's story which you included in the last chapter of Danger Stalks The Land. Once again I thank you for doing such a good job of putting my dad, C.D. Tuggle into print. He deserved something like that and you were the one to do it!

Bear Tales for the Ages

...Larry Kaniut's seventh adventure packed book of outdoor danger; bear attacks, and outdoor lore. It's a cant-put-it-down white knuckle read from page one to the end...28 stories of bear attacks from 1816 to 1999. These were mostly gleaned from his extensive collection of out of print bear books, and rewritten here to introduce a new generation to the wonder of this tenacious animal, and the indomitable spirit of man.

A grizzly bear in Montana ambushes a sheepherder, then there was the man who mounted a "set-gun" to kill a grizzly…bear and bull fights, and a bear and Bull Moose fight in the wild.

Since I, too, live in Alaska, this book has certainly increased my respect for the big bears. They are beautiful animals, but they do not interact well with people. Kaniut's writing is very exciting; he is a premier storyteller, and the action is nonstop.

You can feel the author's anguish when man loses the battle, but the bears are portrayed with respect, awe, and a merged love and fear. Plan to stay up all night to finish this book. You just as well...you are not going to sleep.

Alaska's Fun Bears

Ninety-four fun packed pages for adult-child interaction—designed for adult-child engagement with activities, coloring and information… instead of relegating the younger to Game Boy and another room. Over forty bears dressed and engaged in human outdoor activities— snowboarding, skiing, curling and clamming in Alaska. The book includes alphabet, maze, matching, coloring and tons of questions for the adult to share with the child.

Alaska Air Tales

If you're looking for insight into the world of Alaskan bush pilots you will enjoy this book. It's packed with personal accounts of real experiences written in a page turning way. The mountains, winds, and wilds of Alaska can be very unforgiving for those ill prepared. It's not just a book of machismo moments of thrill seekers. Dr. Bobbie Hemry writes, "After several seconds, a searing pain began in my left shoulder and crescendoed to an intensity that finally made me realize I had been struck by the airplane propeller. Being a physician, my mind made a rapid assessment. Was the blow fatal?" And so the stories go. Paul Claus, with over 28,000 logged hours, gives remarkable insight into unique aspects of mountain flying in Alaska. The book is an excellent addition to anyone's Alaskan aviation library that might already include such books as Wager with the Wind: The Don Sheldon Story and Glacier Pilot.

Amazon reader Alaska Guy, 5 stars, August 3, 2016

Brachan

A Roman soldier, selected to monitor John the Baptist as a threat to the Empire, finds more than one "threat." On his mission Brachan discovers way more than he'd anticipated.

I absolutely love Brachan. You have something very special here. I am amazed. I had no idea you could write like this.

--Randy Mc Kenzie, Bookmasters, email 10-13-15

I often judge a book by the emotions it takes me through. I laughed, I cried a bit, I felt like I was there in the city, on the road with the dust and dirt, there in the temple, your description of the whip, and for the good of Rome, you nailed it, I can't say enough, this is big time to me. I felt like I was there. Your descriptions are very good.

--Randy Mc Kenzie, Bookmasters, email, October 2015

I read Brachan in cold, snowy December and found it so engaging that

it lifted me out of the winter doldrums. Brachan, which means called of God, is a story narrated from the point of view of a Roman soldier who was sent to keep an eye on Jesus lest there be a potential plot brewing to overthrow the Roman empire.

Brachan's accounting of his experience observing the famous Nazarene is so remarkable that the reader actually feels like a back-seat participant in the narrative. This story flows on seamlessly without judgment. While the chronicle regales the last few years of the life of Jesus, it does so sans a preachy tone.

Some of the vivid, detailed descriptions in the book show meticulous research into the era and place where Jesus walked. And the reader gets a good glimpse of the Roman worldview too.

It is a great read and I would recommend it for all audiences—those who enjoy non-fiction as well as those who just like a good plot and story. Brachan is a natural storyteller and once the reader begins, he or she will be hooked to the end.

Amazon reader, 5 stars, Jeanette Prodgers, Dillon, MT, March 19, 2016

Great book!! Larry Kaniut is a wonderful writer in the sense that he can transport his readers to the place and events in the story. You feel as if you are there --hearing the sounds, seeing the action, and even smelling the atmosphere! It is a wonderful, different approach to the events in the life of Jesus Christ. I would recommend this book to anyone- believers as well as nonbelievers.

Amazon reader, Janice Eckard, 5 stars, March 9, 2016

A wonderful read. I just finished your book and had to write you a quick note to tell you how moving and wonderful it was. I am an avid reader, usually spending at least two hours each day reading. A good book is often described as one you can't put down. This often implies that you want to get to the end. Your book was different. I read each page and then often went back and reread sections of the page to fully digest it. I wasn't happy just reading it. I wanted to immerse myself in the details. It is a terrific book Larry. I am so glad that the story doesn't end. I just can't say enough about how really good it is!!!

Amazon reader, August 14, 2016

Trapped

Gabrielle wasn't attempting to save the world but she thought she'd have a chance on her return to New York to shed light on the rights of animals with a photo-journalist piece. What she didn't realize was that her return would be longer than she anticipated.

SAFE with Bears
Coming soon!

Thoroughly documented, latest-best advice for staying out of a bear's mouth.

On the drawing board!

Heavenly Rose
What's Bruin?